THE GIFT OF
Christmas

Cheryl Fosnot Bingisser

ISBN 979-8-88943-365-1 (paperback)
ISBN 979-8-88943-366-8 (digital)

Christian Faith Publishing
832 Park Avenue
Meadville, PA 16335
www.christianfaithpublishing.com

Printed in the United States of America

Presented to: _____

Given by: _____

But I am sure I have always thought of Christmas time, when it has come around…as a good time; a kind, forgiving, charitable, pleasant time; the only time I know of, in the long calendar of the year, when men and women seem by one consent to open their shut-up hearts freely, and to think of people below them as if they really were fellow passengers to the grave, and not another race of creatures bound on other journeys. And therefore, Uncle, though it has never put a scrap of gold or silver in my pocket, I believe that it has done me good, and will do me good, and I say, God bless it!

—Charles Dickens, *A Christmas Carol*

CHAPTER 1

December 1950
Small town in the Rocky Mountain foothills of Colorado

It was the first time Raff had been home in five years, and he wasn't looking forward to it. He smiled as he thought how proud his father might have been if he could've seen him in his '48 Ford. He'd saved for two years for this car knowing how his father loved Fords. He didn't exactly buy it off the showroom's floor, but it was just two years old and in "mint condition" as the salesman called it.

Besides, his father was gone now, and he was coming home to settle the "estate," or so the lawyer called it. He winced as he thought about how long he'd been away. He should have come earlier but didn't. He just didn't want to go through that argument one more time. It always brought anger and disappointment. Anger for him and disappointment for his father.

He'd known since he was a child that his father didn't really love him. There was always something more important to do than spend time with him. It's as though he was invisible, like he didn't exist.

It had started snowing, and he tensed as he focused more on the windy country road ahead.

He dreaded walking through that front door. There were so many ghosts there. Ghosts of Christmases past. Ghosts that he wished would stay buried. To make matters worse, Christmas was just a month away. He didn't have any reason to celebrate, didn't want to, but that's nothing new; they never celebrated Christmas, as least as far back as he could remember.

It seemed his whole life he had tried to make his father proud of him. Like when he made the track team. They had won first place at state, but his father hadn't come to one meet. "Too busy," he said. There were always excuses—none that really made sense, or at least not to him. The lights of an approaching car startled him as he honked and swerved away from Raff, bringing him out of his reverie. He wiped some sweat from his brow and let out a big breath, not realizing he had been holding it. He needed to focus on the road.

The snow had picked up speed, and he was now concerned that if he wasn't careful, he could wind up in a ditch or worse. It was colder out this far in the country, and the temperature dropped ten degrees in just a few minutes. Ice formed quickly and was difficult to detect. He'd seen many accidents on this road in the winter for that very reason. Some didn't survive.

Terry, his best friend since grade school, suffered that fate. He passed away from severe head trauma after he skidded on the ice and ran right into the big oak in the Westemeier's front yard. He didn't stand a chance. The only good thing to come of that was he had just dropped Jenny off, so she wasn't in the car at the time! The whole town came out for the funeral.

His family was devastated. They struggled to make sense of it. He was just seventeen. Just beginning his life that held so much promise. He and Jenny were to be married the following year, a fact about which neither set of parents were thrilled. Terry's parents wanted him to go to college. To become an engineer. Something of which they could be proud. But Terry insisted that they loved each other, and he could always go to school after they got married. They were young and had plenty of time!

Raff shook his head as the memories rolled by. He wanted to stop them. But he didn't seem to have control over them. He didn't want to relive them again. Nothing good came from that! It never settled anything. It only served to put his stomach in knots and his mind fill with grief and remorse.

The snow was piling up fast, and he could hardly see out the windshield. As he turned the corner, he saw a glow. Wait! That was a car with its lights still on. He tried to pull off the road to see if anyone needed help. He skidded off to the side, narrowly missing the ditch, from which the glowing light originated, and finally came to a stop. He opened the car door, and a blast of frigid air struck him as the snow pelted him in the face, making it almost impossible to see. The wind had picked up too, making it harder to stand upright. He stepped gingerly onto the road, careful not to slip on the ice that evidently had formed all over the road. He had to get to that other car to see if there was anyone there. He wasn't exactly prepared for this kind of weather; and his boots, while wildly popular, did nothing to keep his feet from slipping and would probably land him directly on his hip pockets!

When he approached the car, he couldn't see inside the window. He knocked on the window, but no one responded. He tried to open the door, but it seemed stuck.

"Is there anyone in there?" he shouted. "Are you hurt?"

He tried the door again. Nothing. He walked around the front to the passenger side. He could see that the door was perched up on the side of the ditch and knew there was no way he was going to get that door opened. *Now what do I do?* he thought. *I've got to see if anyone is in there and maybe hurt.*

He tried the other doors, but they seemed to be locked. The only thing he could think of to do was to drive to the closest neighbor that wasn't that far away, and borrow a crowbar or something that could aid in opening a car door.

CHAPTER 2

Old Man Strattford didn't answer the door so Raff hoped it would be okay if he borrowed something from the barn. Strattford wasn't exactly friendly to anyone but seemed to especially hate kids. Course, that only made it more fun to torture him with all kinds of pranks, always making things more tense and very unneighborly. They didn't think they really did anything too awful but knew from the beginning it was not the right thing to do.

"What would Jesus do?" his mother used to ask him. He really didn't get into all the Jesus stuff. What had Jesus ever done for him? He never answered any of his prayers. How many nights had he tearfully prayed on his bed at night for God to make his father love him? That obviously never worked. He never saved Terry. *Why would I believe that Jesus would do anything for me now?* he thought. Praying was useless! Believing that Jesus loved him was about as ridiculous as believing his father did.

Now, Mom was a different story. She went to church every Sunday, carried her Bible, memorized Bible verses, and tried to get Raff to memorize along with her. She volunteered at the community center, sang in the choir, even taught third-grade Sunday school class. On Tuesdays she read to an elderly woman up the street who was a shut-in, to whom she often brought a meal. Raff even overheard his mother pray for him occasionally. He never understood that, but what did it matter? In the end, what good did it do her? She died of pancreatic cancer, a slow and painful death. All the prayers in the world didn't help her. No, Jesus was just a crutch that weak people used to try to make themselves feel better. It certainly wasn't for him.

He sighed as he searched for some kind of tool he could use. It took a while for his eyes to adjust to the darkness. Even with the car lights aimed at the barn, it was hard to focus. "There! A crowbar," he said under his breath. He grabbed it and made his way back to the car.

The shot startled him as the bullet whizzed by his ear! Raff hit the dirt.

"Who goes there!" Strattford gruffly shouted.

"Hold your fire! It's me, Raff!" He slowly stood up with his hands in the air.

"What are you doing out there, boy?"

"I'm borrowing a crowbar. There's an accident about a mile back, and I needed something to get into the car to see if anyone's hurt," he reasoned.

"Raff! What are you doing home? Oh, yeah," he remembered. "Sorry to hear about your dad," he said sympathetically.

First, Raff thought that sounded unlike the Old Man Strattford he knew and disliked, but since he didn't have time to discuss it further, he thanked him and said he would be on his way. Second, Strattford was a good shot; he was surprised he didn't wake up dead! Then again, if Strattford wanted him dead, he would be. As he walked toward the car, he turned back and said he would return the crowbar as soon as he could.

By now there was about four inches of snow on the road, and he needed to get back as soon as possible. Someone might need to get to the hospital. He wished he would have told Strattford to call for an ambulance but wasn't sure if anyone needed one.

As he was getting closer to the car, the snowflakes got bigger and blurred his vision. He looked over the steering wheel trying to concentrate on the road and looking for ice so the same fate didn't befall him as it did the other unfortunate soul.

He parked in front of the car, leaving the lights on. Grabbing the crowbar, he walked to the driver's door. Squeezing the crowbar inside, he pried and pushed, but absolutely nothing budged. He tried again. Nothing. He summoned every ounce of strength he had, and the door creaked as it began to move. He took a deep breath and pushed again. It moved. Just a mite. Another deep breath, and he pushed again. It groaned as it shifted to the left. Raff grunted as he tried again. Finally, it popped open. Dropping the crowbar, his mind raced as he tried to wrap his head around the scene in front of him.

The back seat was full of boxed and brightly wrapped Christmas presents. Christmas! He shook his head as if to bring himself to and tried to concentrate on the woman in the driver's seat. Oozing blood from her temple and seeing the goose egg already forming, he grabbed his handkerchief from his trousers pocket and pressed it against her head. It didn't look too bad, but she was still unconscious, and that worried him. He quickly and discreetly surveyed the rest of her body for any breaks or other injuries and found none.

"Ma'am! Ma'am! Are you okay?" He lightly shook her to arouse her without any further damage. "You must wake up! Please," he pleaded. Leaning her back against the seat, he spoke softly to her. Her eyes started to flutter open.

"Ma'am, are you all right?" he questioned.

She nodded slowly.

"How many fingers do you see?"

"Three? I think three."

"Good," he whispered.

"Raff, is that you?"

His eyes narrowed. Staring, he tried to remember how she might know him.

"Raff. It's me, Maddie!"

With his eyes as big as saucers, he studied her.

Finally dawning on him, he asked, "Maddie?"

"It's me, Raff," she replied softly.

"Maddie, are you all right?"

"I have a pretty bad headache," she said as she touched her temple.

"Ouch!" she yelped.

Raff chuckled. "You've got a pretty bad bump on your head. Are you sure you're okay?"

She nodded, a little embarrassed.

"Yeah, I'm fine...other than freezing, and the headache, of course," she admitted.

"What happened?"

Her lips curled up. "I just slipped off the road. I guess I must have hit some ice or something."

"Well, you shouldn't have been driving in the snow!" he said tersely.

Protesting a little louder than she needed, she said, "It wasn't snowing when I started out!"

"Whatever, we should probably get you to a doctor and get you checked out," he said, as if to dismiss her.

She felt like a student just getting lectured by the principal. She turned her head and stared out the other window. Water pooled in her eyes. She quickly wiped them away. She would not cry. Not in front of Raff. *I'm not going to give him the satisfaction,* she thought angrily.

Just as quickly as the anger came, it was gone and left grief in its wake. That was a far more familiar emotion anyway. She'd lived with that ever since Raff left five years ago. She tried to move on. She was even engaged once. But the truth was that she'd always been in love with Raff—and him only. He just acted like she was his kid sister and certainly not a viable girlfriend.

He was moody and often short-tempered. She never really understood that. She did know that he'd come from a rough home life. So many times, she tried to comfort him and tell him about Jesus. He was the only one that could understand him fully and love him beyond anything he could ever imagine. But he wouldn't hear of it! He was never interested in spiritual things. She had even invited him to youth group and outings, but his answer was always a definite "Never!"

She sighed. She was always just going to be "his little friend" from next door. She cringed as all those memories came flooding back. Would it always hurt so badly? When would she ever be able to move on?

"Maddie, are you sure you're okay?" he asked softly.

Realizing that he was speaking to her, she answered curtly.

"I'm fine, but I'm not sure my car is."

"Let's not worry about that right now. I don't want you driving home anyway."

She acquiesced and nodded.

"Let's get you to the hospital and make sure that bump on your head isn't going to leave a lasting impression." He laughed.

Swooping her up, he walked her over to his car and gently placed her into the passenger seat. Of course, she protested the whole way, but Raff ignored her. He needed to make sure she was not going to have any repercussions from that accident. She needed a thorough look-see, and he certainly wasn't the one to give it to her. He wanted a doctor's opinion before he would take her home. He would make sure she was safely home and tucked in—if that's what it took.

He went back to Maddie's car and turned off the lights and locked the door, making a mental note to get those gifts out soon. But not now. She was most important; the rest could wait.

CHAPTER 3

After the doctor had a good look at her, and deemed her able to leave the hospital, they headed home. He did give her strict instructions to get some rest for the next couple of days before resuming regular activities.

The ride home was a quiet one. Raff was concentrating on the road. Even though the snow had stopped, the road was still icy, and the temperature had not improved. Maddie was lost in her own thoughts and didn't want to interfere with Raff's concentration. She already knew how dangerous the roads were and didn't want a repeat performance of her earlier mishap.

It took much longer than expected, and Maddie dozed with her head against the window. Raff glanced over at her and grinned as he recalled how defensive she was when he spoke to her about driving in the snow. When had she gotten so beautiful, or was she always like that, and he just hadn't noticed? She certainly filled out in all the right places. He tried not to think about it while he was carrying her, but he was very much aware she was all woman now. But he couldn't get involved with anyone; he had a lot of work to do. A lot to sort through. He was certain his father had left him with a huge mess to clean up, and he dreaded going through all of it!

He glanced at her and saw she was sleeping as her chest was lightly moving up and down. He turned back to the road. *Concentrate, Raff,* he scolded himself. She certainly made it difficult.

She stirred as he turned into her driveway.

"Are we home?" she murmured.

"Yes, you are," he said as he smiled at her. "Stay right there, and I'll get you into the house."

"I can walk," she demanded.

"Not on my watch," he pronounced. "Now stay put and not another word!"

"Demanding, aren't we?" Her lips curled in amusement.

"I can be, when it's warranted," he said, trying not to smile. She thought she detected the beginning of a curl on one side of his mouth, which finally broke into a full-blown grin. He smiled back at her, trying not to laugh. *She is a scrappy one*, he thought.

They got to the front porch, which was straddled by columns and a huge wrap-around deck. He'd forgotten how beautiful this old house was. At least they kept it up, so it maintained its former beauty. He admired that. Something his father never did.

He helped her stand, and they walked into the house. He made sure she was situated before asking if she could undress and get herself to bed.

"Of course," she replied.

He bid her good night and left. He stood on the porch shaking his head. *That woman will be my undoing.*

Move on, Raff, he chided himself. It was time to go home and face the music.

CHAPTER 4

H e turned up the drive and put it into park, turned off the motor, and just sat there. He raked his hand through his hair. He wished he didn't have to go in there.

"You can't sit here forever," he whispered. "How do I do this?" he wondered. "Where do I even start?" He walked into the house. He glanced at the clock on the wall and saw it was midnight, and he resolved to start in the morning. There was only so much one could pack into one day, and he was exhausted. Just thinking about what lay in front of him gave him the shivers, or was it because there wasn't any heat on in the house? He quickly got a fire roaring in the fireplace, leaving the bedroom door opened to warm it, undressed, and climbed into bed. His bones ached; he was so tired. But he was wide awake. He lay there for an hour before he gave up, and went into the living room and sat in the wingbacked chair close to the fireplace.

He perused the books in the bookcase in the living room and found an old copy of *A Christmas Carol*. He read it as a kid, but maybe it was worth another look-see. After all, it was Christmas. Not that he cared about that. But when he didn't see anything else that interested him, he began reading.

"Chapter one. Marley was dead to begin with!" *Kind of creepy*, he thought. But he also knew it had to do with ghosts, and he had plenty of those of his own. He wondered how Scrooge dealt with them. He knew he could use a few pointers at the very least. He read on. Just a few sentences later…

"Dead as a doornail!"

"Still creepy." He smiled.

Maybe this isn't the time to read this anyway. He yawned and stretched. Maybe he could sleep now. He put a couple smaller logs on the fire and strode toward the bedroom. He undressed, slipped between the sheets, and started to relax. His last thoughts turned to Maddie. He chuckled to himself.

She is something special, all right, he mused as he drifted off to a deep sleep.

CHAPTER 5

Maddie thought about walking to her bedroom. Now that she was on her own, she didn't have to walk upstairs, a thought that brought considerable relief tonight. Her headache was raging, a truth that she would never share with Raff. She didn't want him to think she was too delicate. She was strong. She could do anything most men could do. She had run her parents' farm after they were killed in a bad accident.

They weren't expecting the snowfall as her folks headed up the mountain to visit Gram Betsy. After all, it started out with a crystal-blue sky and a lot of pure, beautiful sunshine. The weather report hailed clear skies, so everything seemed fine. Until the worst snowfall in several years roared through the mountain pass. They were going slowly enough, the officer thought, but they must have hit some black ice and skidded right over the cliff, probably killing them instantly. After that, her maternal grandmother, Ruby, moved in with Maddie and raised her until she passed away just two years ago. So at eighteen, she was on her own again. She missed Grammy Ruby very much, but it was always her mother over whom she shed tears.

She realized that her face was wet again. She hated that! But even though it happened ten years ago, it still hurt. She still missed them very much. The ache of the loss and the loneliness left a huge hole in her heart that never seemed to entirely heal.

She started to stand up, and dizziness gripped her. The room started spinning, and nausea began in her stomach. She grabbed the arm of the couch to steady herself. Her head throbbed. She needed to get to the bathroom. The nausea spread up in her throat. She gulped and gasped for air. She swallowed as the nausea finally subsided. Her feet felt unsteady, like the floor was falling away.

"Lord Jesus, what is happening?"

Frightened, she quickly sat down. Remembering something her mother told her, she put her head between her knees and breathed deeply. Her head started to clear. The floor stopped waving, and the spinning slowed to a halt. She thanked God. Maybe she could survive this night after all, which had looked doubtful just a few moments ago. She sat still a few more minutes before heading toward the bedroom. She slowly and methodically undressed and slipped on her nightgown. The room was cold, so she left her socks on to keep her feet warm. She abhorred cold feet. Once her feet were cold, her whole body was frigid. She placed an extra blanket on the bottom of the bed from the top shelf of the closet. It was the quilt that her mother made for her when she turned ten.

"That's a very special age," her mother told her. Maddie smiled as she remembered how her mother glowed with pride when she gave it to her that day. She couldn't wait to place it on her bed. She loved it so. She ran her fingers over the patches that came from old clothes she'd worn in the past. Such sweet memories.

"Mom, I miss you," she whispered. "God, tell her I said hi and how very much I miss her. Oh, and while I'm praying, can you help Raff? He has so much to deal with, and he doesn't have you to help him through it. Lord, please bring him to you. Help him see how very much you love him. And while you're at it, can you help him see how very much I love him too? Thank you for loving me. In Jesus's name, amen."

She fluffed her pillow and softly laid her head down.

"Ouch!" she cried. She touched her head.

"Wow! That bump isn't getting any smaller, and neither is the headache," she whined. Even so, she drifted off to sleep with Raff's laugh still in her heart and a smile pasted on her lips.

CHAPTER 6

At forty-two, Franklin Atwood limped toward the barn. Since he sold his cattle, all he had left to do was take care of the land and see that the garden and the orchard were ready for spring. With six inches of snow on the ground, that was one thing he could cross off his list. Actually, now that he was outside, the bitter cold went all the way through to his bones. His leg burned with pain. He hated that it made him feel lesser than other men. He saw the way both men and women looked at him and knew they pitied him. Kids teased him, but he ignored them.

Doc had given him some liniment to rub on it to help with the pain, but it didn't really work well during the winter months. He offered him pain medication, but Franklin was afraid of becoming dependent upon it. He'd seen that happen in the war and wasn't about to go through that. So he managed as well as could be expected.

With Pearl gone for three years now, three Christmases, he only had to care for himself. She died of influenza. No one thought it was going to be that bad, but it swept through their little town like wildfire. There was nothing he could do. The doctor was spread thin, and Franklin lived quite a way out of town. In the winter, it was rough traveling.

Christmas was always a hard time for him. Pearly, as he called her, used to decorate with greens on the mantle, sprinkled with holly and candles. She made him cut down a blue spruce every Christmas and would decorate it with popcorn and cranberries and colored lights. And topped with an angel that was made by Franklin's mother.

It was beautiful to behold, and her face glowed like a beautiful sunset. She thrived in its elegance and festiveness. Sitting in the rocker he had made for her, she would read her Bible aloud. Franklin thought that was fine, but he never truly understood how reading the Bible brought her so much joy. Still, if it made her happy, he was all right with it.

Sitting in her rocker, the memories rolled by while he lit his pipe. She used to love the sweet smell as it hung in the air. He rested his head against the back of the chair and slipped off to a restless sleep.

He awoke with a jerk when his pipe hit his knee. That could have been bad news. Maybe it was time to go to bed. He hated to go into that room without his Pearly. He put his pipe away. Sighing, he closed his eyes and drifted off.

CHAPTER 7

The sun poured in through the bedroom window. Raff's eyes fluttered open and then slammed shut. He was not ready for sunshine. He rolled over onto his side and tried to go back to sleep. There's no way that was happening. He looked around and remembered where he was. Sighing, he sat up and put his feet on the floor. A chill ran through him. He got dressed and put some warm socks on in lieu of slippers and sauntered out to the living room to start a fire. He put his boots and coat on and went outside to chop wood. He had thought about it last night but was way too tired to expend that kind of energy.

His thoughts turned to Maddie and wondered how she was doing. Nope, couldn't do that. He had to stop thinking about her. No distractions. All he wanted to do was sell this farm and get back to his real life—whatever that was going to look like. He sure didn't want to stay in this one-horse town. He left this town behind him years ago, and that's where it was going to stay—behind him!

He always thought his father wasn't really a first-rate farmer. He had inherited the apple orchard from his grandfather who had done well. When Raff's dad took over, he tried hard, and they did eke out a living, but nothing ever to spare and nothing for Raff at all. If he made more money than that, he never shared it.

He looked down at his boots. *I've got to get some boots that actually do more than look impressive,* he thought as he shook his head. *These things will get me killed!*

He chopped a couple loads of wood and headed into the house. He put some bigger logs on the fire and wandered to the kitchen to find some coffee. He searched the cupboards. Next the fridge. Nothing.

"What in the world did he eat?" he queried. He decided to head into town, buy some groceries, and walk to the shoe store for some boots. He stopped at the General Store and threw in some coffee, eggs, milk, cheese, and bread. "At least I can fix myself a good break-fast," he muttered. He looked around a little bit more and decided that a toaster would be a good investment, so he threw that in the cart as well.

Maybe I should stop by on my way home and check on Maddie, he reasoned. *After all, she was in an accident, and someone should check on her. I am the closest, and she would be more comfortable with me than someone else.* He knew in his heart he was just trying to rationalize a visit, but it was semi-legit, right?

He drove slowly and saw the neighbor's new huge Christmas display in the front yard. There was a six-foot Santa with eight rein-deer plus Rudolf, a nativity scene complete with a stable, and every one of the characters, including angels. There were elves, wrapped Christmas presents in neon lighting, and several decorated Christmas trees with lights strung everywhere—a little something for everyone.

He just didn't get why anyone would put so much stuff in the front yard. He certainly wasn't impressed. But Christmas wasn't his thing anyway. So why did it bother him so much? It just looked cheap and overdone. He shook his head as he turned into Maddie's driveway.

What was he doing here? *I should leave before she sees me,* he thought. Too late. She looked out the window. Raff waved at her as he got out of the car and walked up to the front door. She was wait-ing for him. She checked herself in the mirror before she opened the door. Her hair could use some work, but there was no time.

"Hi, Raff, won't you come in?"

He nodded. "Sure, thanks."

"Come in and have a seat." She smiled.

He turned and walked toward the chair. *Good grief, that woman even looks attractive in the morning,* he thought as he quickly turned away.

"Would you like some coffee? I have some on the stove."

"I really can't stay, I just wanted to come by and see how you are doing," he told her. Even to him he didn't sound convincing. Oh, how he wanted to stay and spend some time with her. But he knew that wouldn't be a good idea. He had to keep to his plan. No distractions.

"How are you, Maddie?" he inquired. "How's your head? It looks like the swelling's gone down some. How's your headache?" *Slow down,* he told himself. He was starting to sound like a magpie.

"It's a little better today, but not totally gone," she said, amused by his awkwardness. "At least it's not throbbing like it did last night." She smiled as she touched her temple, wincing.

"Still sore, I bet."

"Yes, a little." She giggled. "Okay, a lot sore," she admitted.

Raff laughed. "I'm sorry, Maddie. Is there anything I can do for you before I leave? Remember, the doctor told you to rest today," he scolded.

"I know," she said, not totally on board with lying on the couch with her feet up all day. "You know I've never been very good at sitting still," she retorted with a fetching smile.

He found himself searching her eyes—those beautiful jade eyes a man could get lost in—and then slowly lowered them to her lips, where they lingered. He even entertained the idea of kissing her, wondering what that would feel like… Her tight, curly red hair fell against her back beyond her shoulders, displaying her Irish heritage. Her eyes and hair, she inherited from her father; but her nose and mouth—all her mother's. That cute, little turned-up nose, and that mouth that made the sweetest little bow. *How dare she turn into this amazing woman! So irritating!* He liked it better when he thought of her as a kid sister.

They had always been friends, even though he was five years older than she. They spent a lot of time in the tree house sharing their hopes and dreams. Maddie had always been more mature than her age would dictate; maybe he just hadn't given her as much credit as she deserved. The age difference didn't seem such a barrier anymore. That scared him a little. No. That scared him a lot. That and that peaches-and-cream complexion. Flawless, yet not made up or fake like some girls from the city. She had a natural beauty that was downright stunning.

What in the world was he thinking? He had to shake her from his mind if he was ever to get anything done today.

She looked at him demurely. *Why is he staring at me?* she wondered. *Does he know how irresistibly attractive he is? He must, if he has a mirror in his house*, she surmised. His sandy, blond hair was always a little tousled but extremely attractive. He had the most enchanting blue eyes that she could swim in, but felt he could see into her very soul. She'd have to be a better actress if she didn't want him to know what she was thinking. That unnerved her. She thought she detected his eyes on her mouth. Was he about to kiss her? One could only hope so. Nope, his eyes turned away.

She was sure he still thought of her as a sister. Would he ever see her for who she was now? She was not a little girl anymore. Disappointment flickered across her eyes for just a second, and then resumed their sparkle that was so charming.

"I better get moving," he said with relief. "I have so much to do, and I'm not even sure where to start, but I can't put it off any longer."

"I'm sorry, Raff. Is there anything I can do to help?" she asked sympathetically.

"I'm afraid not. I just have to get into Dad's office and go through all the paperwork and find out what sad state of affairs the farm is really in," he said sadly. "Besides, your only job today is to rest like Doc told you to," he said conspiratorially.

"Yes, yes, I know. But, Raff, why don't you stop by for dinner tonight? I'll fix something simple so it's not too taxing, and you can take a much-needed break."

"Well, I… I guess that would be okay…but only if you promise not to spend too long slaving over a hot stove." He softly laughed.

"I won't. I promise." Her eyes danced as she smiled her most irresistible smile.

His laughter was music to her ears.

"Okay then, I've got to run. You take care now, you hear?" He walked out the door and down the steps to the car.

How is it she keeps doing that to me? She's beautiful, charming, smart, giving, and joyful, and it is totally irresistible! he thought, shaking his head. A smile crossed his face, and he quickly quelled it. He had work to do. He had to get his head in the game. He took a deep breath, not knowing for sure what awaited him. He'd much rather stay here and talk with Maddie but knew that was impossible.

CHAPTER 8

Raff placed his hand on the doorknob to his dad's office. He sighed as his shoulders slumped. For just an instant, he wished he were a praying man. Then he quickly dismissed the thought and walked through the door.

The papers covered the desk. He was sure there was a desk under there somewhere. Hard to tell. He raked his hand through his hair. A heavy sigh brushed past his lips. *May as well get started. These papers aren't going to take care of themselves*, he mused.

His eyes darted around the room. They rested on the floor-to-ceiling bookcase filled with what looked like first edition books. He ran his fingers over some of the titles and picked up a lot of dust for his effort.

How could Dad ever afford first edition books? he wondered. *We never had any money.* At least not that he remembered. *He certainly hadn't spent any on Mom or me*, he thought. He glanced again at some of the titles. *War and Peace, Little Women, A Christmas Carol.* He stopped. *Really? Scrooge again. What is it with that story that seems to sit on so many bookshelves?* he questioned. He moved on. *The Red Badge of Courage, Moby Dick. How eclectic*, he thought. There was a wide range of titles that Raff glanced through with wonder. He never was much of a reader, but these were classics. He knew enough to know that much at least. Intrigued by it all, he thought, *Maybe I should give reading a try.*

But wait! How and when had this all happened? He'd never seen them before. These must have cost a fortune. Where had the money come from? Nothing made sense. His brows furrowed as he tried to think logically. His mind went back to his childhood, and the memories blew by like one of those movies he'd been to. Nothing came to mind that would warrant all this. He pinched his nose. *What had Dad gotten himself into? Surely if they were stolen, they wouldn't be displayed in a bookcase in a room that had no lock. So, just what was the deal?* The longer he thought about it, the more confused he got. His head started pounding. *Great*, he glowered. *I wonder if Dad has any aspirin anywhere*, he questioned.

He walked into the bathroom to the medicine cabinet. He searched for a bottle he recognized. "There. That's it." He grabbed it and started to close the door when his eye went to the prescriptions lined up on the second shelf. He wondered what his dad was taking. He knew two of them had to do with his heart, which made sense since he died of a massive heart attack. But what was this one? He hadn't heard of it before, but maybe that was just another blood thinner or something. He shrugged his shoulders, closed the door, and walked into the kitchen for a glass to take the aspirin. He filled his glass with water and swallowed them down. Two should do it. Maybe three. He took another one. He placed the glass in the sink and moved toward the office again. All the questions resurfaced. He shook his head.

"*I'll deal with all that later. Right now I need to get through all those papers*," he thought, as he chastened himself.

He walked behind the desk and sat in the old wooden chair. *You would think after all these years, he could have gotten a comfortable leather chair. Maybe sell a book*, he thought angrily.

He picked up the paper on the top. It was a receipt for the horses he had sold five years ago—right before Raff left home. He even sold Sport, his favorite horse and companion. He would ride for hours, and Sport would unleash his power and run like the wind. Raff reveled in his spirit and freedom the speed brought him. It was the only time he felt totally free. Free from his father, free from expectations, free from his teachers, free from everything. He loved that horse, and the memories of it brought anger and resentment to his heart. It still hurt, and he would never forgive his father for the pain he had inflicted upon him. Course, the horse was just the final hurt in a long line of them. A lifetime really. But no sense dwelling on that now, he had to get to the project at hand. He wished he were finished with all of it. He needed to leave this farm and all its bad memories.

He looked at the clock. Time had flown by, and maybe he was ready for a break. It was six in the evening, after all. Maybe Maddie had dinner ready. He hoped she hadn't overdone it. He worried about that. But she did promise to take it easy, so he hoped she had kept her promise to him.

He flipped off the light and walked to the door. Grabbing his coat from the peg on the wall and putting on his new work boots, he stepped through the door. He couldn't wait to see Maddie. He really shouldn't feel this way about her, but he just couldn't help himself. She was just too darn pretty and charming. Too much so for his own good. But he tucked those thoughts away to deal with them later. For now, he was going to enjoy every moment of being with her. He loved her feminine giggle and the way she wrinkled up her nose when she was irritated. The thoughts of her made him chuckle. She was a challenge for sure, but one he was likely going to enjoy. He could handle anything she could dish out. Oh yes, he was definitely up for the challenge.

CHAPTER 9

Maddie went to the bathroom mirror and pinned up her hair in a curly roll. She left a few curls on the sides. She dressed in a burgundy blouse with a tie that made into a bow at the neck. It was one of her favorite colors. She thought it made her eyes sparkle. The skirt was knee-length with a black background and burgundy flowers. Looking in the full-length mirror, she took off the apron, threw it on the bed, and pressed down her skirt. Twirling, to make sure the back looked as good as her front, she nodded with satisfaction and walked out the bedroom door into the kitchen.

The smells from the oven made her stomach growl. *Where is he?* she wondered. She pulled out the roaster and lifted the lid. She breathed in the scent. The beef roast, red potatoes, and carrots combined to make the best aroma. It was always one of her favorites growing up. Her mom was a great cook and took pride in her prowess in the kitchen.

She took a fork and poked the roast. Done. Then the potatoes and carrots. Also done. She put the lid back on and slid the roaster back in the oven and turned it off. She sighed, wondering if he was going to show up at all. A knock on the door interrupted her thoughts.

She walked quickly to the door. Looking briefly in the mirror, she pinned up a stray curl and opened the door. There he was looking every bit the gentleman—and so handsome too. A lock of blond hair fell over his forehead, and quickly brushed it back. An old habit she recognized from years back. So very becoming. Oh, how she loved him.

He looked at her, waiting for an invitation, when she realized she'd been staring. She cleared her throat.

"Ah, um…please, come in." Red came from her neck and spread all the way to her face. She forced herself to calm down and hoped Raff hadn't noticed. She looked in his eyes and saw the sparkle and the smile on his face. She could tell he was trying to stifle a chuckle at her expense.

He did notice, she realized. That only made the blush redder. She turned away as she motioned for him to come in and take a seat. He nodded and walked through the door to the wingbacked chair by the fireplace where a fire was warming the room. He threw his coat over the back of the chair and sat down.

"Something smells awfully good," he offered, finally letting her off the hook. "Are you sure you didn't overdo it today?" he asked.

"I assure you I did not, sir," Maddie said crossly. There must be a way to restore her dignity.

"Sir?" He grinned.

"Well, if you're going to treat me like a child, I guess my response should sound like a child," she said. The moment she let those words escape her lips, she wished she could take them back. She knew she had overreacted.

Raff's brow raised. "Oh, I see. I just wanted to make sure you kept your promise, and from the smells coming from the kitchen, I'm not sure you did," he said sternly.

Immediately, her mood changed, and he saw regret cross her face. She searched his face and saw his lips start to curl up at the sides and then broke into laughter.

"Maddie, I was teasing you."

She responded with her most endearing giggle.

So feminine, he thought.

"How about we eat at the kitchen table," she offered.

He nodded. "Sounds good to me."

They walked into the kitchen. The walls were a soft yellow. There was a small fridge and range with a space on the side to put hot food. The cupboards were white, and the table was an old oblong dark walnut, with a floral tablecloth. It was a homey kitchen with warmth, inviting guests to enjoy conversation. It was small, but enough room for four if they cuddled a little. He almost wished there were four people here so he would have an excuse to cuddle with her.

Maddie stepped over to the stove and pulled the roaster out of the oven while Raff scraped a chair across the floor and took a seat. She placed it on the empty space and removed the lid. She stepped over to the cupboard to retrieve a platter. Taking a serving fork from the silverware drawer, she moved to the stove and began serving dinner. She took two plates from the cupboard and pulled two forks, two spoons, and two knives from the same silverware drawer and placed one plate in front of Raff and one directly across from him. Putting the silverware in place at the sides of each plate, she wondered why she hadn't set the table earlier. She certainly had enough time.

She knew the answer was that she couldn't focus on anything but Raff. She had worn a path in the living room carpet waiting for him to arrive. Realizing she had forgotten the napkins, she opened the drawer below the silverware and pulled out two white cloth napkins, folded them, and placed them beside the plates.

She placed the platter in the middle of the table and poured each of them a glass of water. She left the serving fork on the platter so Raff could help himself and then bowed her head to say grace.

Raff looked at her. He should have seen it coming, but it had been a long time since he'd been anywhere where grace was spoken. He bowed his head as Maddie began to pray. Raff looked up and studied her. She was so beautiful and innocent. When had that changed for him, or maybe he never was innocent? As far back as he could remember, he felt like his innocence was a thing of years past. He did know he never wanted to do anything to hurt her. Nothing to change that sweet, innocent face of hers. Maybe that was another reason to stay away from her, but could he, really? He vaguely heard her end with an amen and pretended to have his eyes closed.

She looked up as Raff opened his eyes. He served himself and then began eating as she was dishing up her own plate. The conversation was easy and light. It almost felt like it did when they were kids. Back when they could talk about anything. There was a lot of laughter that rang through the kitchen as they talked of old times.

She looked up from her plate with a furrowed brow and hurt in her eyes. Raff wondered what was going on in her head. Something was certainly bothering her. Maybe she wasn't feeling well and needed to lie down.

With concern in his eyes, he studied her. "Maddie, are you okay? Did you do too much? Do you need to lie down," he asked softly.

"No, it's nothing like that." She waited until her voice would hold steady.

"Maddie, what is it?"

"I… I…just wondered…"

"Wondered what?" he pleaded. "Please tell me."

"I wondered why you left town so suddenly without even saying goodbye or where you were going."

Raff groaned. That's the last thing he wanted to get into tonight. His head dropped. *Why did she have to bring that up now?* he wondered.

"Maddie, do we really have to get into this now?" he asked, pleading with her not to pursue it further.

She studied him as water began pooling in her eyes.

"Just please help me understand, Raff. How could you do that? To your parents. To me. How? Help me understand. Please…"

He shook his head.

"Look, Maddie, I just can't talk about it yet, okay?"

He placed his hand over hers, and a tingle ran up her spine. He wasn't angry, but he still had things to work through and just wasn't ready to share it. Now, how to tell her something that will satisfy her for the moment. "I still have things… I'm sorry. I just can't." He studied her for a minute.

"Maybe it's time for me to go." He scraped his chair against the wood floor and stood.

Walking toward the front door, he grabbed his coat and stopped. He turned toward her with his hand on the doorknob.

"Thank you for dinner, Maddie. I really am sorry. I hope you will try and understand," he said with concern and regret in his eyes.

With that said, he opened the door and walked out of the house, leaving Maddie staring at the door with tears in her eyes.

He strode down the steps feeling depressed. That's certainly not the way he wanted this evening to end. He didn't want to talk about his dad or the things he'd done wrong. If he told her what sins he had committed, he would never see her again. That would make things easier, but he wasn't really wanting to stop seeing her. He wasn't even sure he could. He was crazy about her, but there was no future for them if he didn't get some things straightened out. Future? Since when did he start thinking of a future with her? The more he thought about it, the more he liked the idea. Then immediately slammed the door on those thoughts and drove home.

CHAPTER 10

It had started snowing again, and the temperature plummeted. Franklin added more wood on the fire as the wind found its way through the tiny cracks between the logs of his three-room cabin. He needed to fix them, soon. Pearly was content with their home the way it was, and it suited him fine. There were just the two of them. They were never able to have kids, a fact that hurt for many years. They each blamed themselves for the absence of children. But they finally got past it and went on with life. Pearly used to say that the Bible said they needed to be content with what they had. So they were.

There was no doubt they loved each other. No one really saw Franklin the way Pearly did. She saw through the gruffness and the long rough beard to the teddy bear he was on the inside. The exterior was only to hide his fear of being hurt again, and his history was responsible for that.

His childhood was a rough one. His father believed intensely that "you spare the rod, you spoil the child." It is in the Bible, but he took it to the extreme. There wasn't anything Franklin could do to please his dad. He didn't stop with the children, either. After drinking, his cruelty became more malicious and he would unleash his wrath on his mother, too.

Pearly really understood him. Course, no one else knew of his history. She was the only one with whom he shared those intimate details of his life. No one else needed to be in his business. That's private and needed to stay that way.

"Yep, Pearly was one of a kind." He smiled lovingly. She used to say that he called her Pearly just for those pearly gates where St. Peter stood. If that made her happy, he was willing to go along with it. She was sweet, kind, and loving. She was always giving to other people in need. Often, he would come in from the orchard, and she would have several women in for Bible study. That's when he poured himself a fresh cup of coffee and headed to the barn. Who wanted to listen to a bunch of hens squawking? He certainly didn't. There's much better company in the barn, even if it's only Barney, the cat. He was a mouser and stayed outside, which made him pretty good company when Franklin expelled himself to the outdoors.

He trusted her with everything. How he wished he could have just five more minutes with her. He would tell how much he loved her and how he would protect her with everything in him. But she would say that she knew that because he already did.

"Oh, Pearly, how I miss you," he whispered. A tear escaped from his eye, and he didn't even bother to wipe it away.

The action he regretted most was when he left his mom and dad and ran away. Pearl Harbor had just been bombed, and that was his escape route. He ran immediately to the recruiting office and enlisted in the army. Maybe if he had found a way to protect her while he was gone, he wouldn't feel so guilty. But he knew that would have been impossible. That was something he would have to live with for the rest of his life. Hindsight was something he'd learned never changed things, so he had to let it go.

He was sent to the South Pacific, where some of the fighting was the worst. They had been searching for land mines, which the Japanese excelled in burying. He stepped lightly and heard the click. Then all he remembered was the flash of light, the blast, and the pain. It took part of his leg. They were able to save the knee, but the rest was gone.

A few weeks later, he was fitted for a prosthetic. Really, it was a wooden leg with leather straps to tie it to the leg and the wiring around the top of the stump. Even though very small strides had been made in that regard, it wasn't enough to suit him. But if he wanted to walk again, and he did, he needed to use it no matter how much he hated it.

He never really got used to his artificial leg. The flesh would bleed after a hard day's work, and the pain could be excruciating. Maybe that was God's way of punishing him. Even though he didn't really believe in God. Too much pain in the world. Too many wars. Too many orphans. Why, if God was love, didn't he do something about the destruction and death in this old world? No, even if he wanted to believe, there was too much evidence to the contrary. He got along just fine without him.

He couldn't show her when the pain was at its worst. He didn't want Pearly to pity him or feel sorry for him. He hated that!

But Pearly always knew when his pain was severe. She never let on, not wanting to embarrass him. He was a proud man and she wanted to preserve his dignity. It would remain her secret, and she would take it to her grave.

He had planted a twenty-acre pear orchard fifteen years ago, and even though he had years that were less than perfect, he had made a profit and was enjoying that part of the farm. Spring and summer were hard, but the winter brought rest since there wasn't a whole lot to do with snow on the ground. The real work began in earnest in early spring, and from then until after the harvest, there were always things to do—and many things that could blow the whole season, and he'd lose everything. But the last few years had been fairly good, and he was comfortable. He had everything he needed.

CHAPTER 11

Walking down the boarded walkway, Kathleen Brennan wasn't paying any attention to what was going on around her.

She had a few packages in her arms and was headed for the General Store. Staring at the meager inventory in the windows, and wishing that could change, she ran right into him. Her packages fell every which way.

"Why don't you watch where you're going, you...you brute!" she shouted.

"Me, watch where I'm going? You're the one who ran into me!" he barked.

"I beg your pardon, sir, but it is you who is at fault!"

Bending over, Franklin started to pick up the packages as she watched him.

"Well, aren't you going to help?"

"Why should I? It's your fault!"

He looked at her and shook his head. *Women!* he thought. He handed her the packages. He started to walk away, and she grabbed his arm.

"Aren't you going to apologize?" she demanded.

"Fine. Anything to get you out of the way so I can get on with my errands, ma'am. I apologize." He bowed low and feigned regret.

"Fine!"

"Fine!"

She sashayed on down the walk. He watched her walk away. It wasn't entirely a bad view. She was well-dressed, with an elegant hat. But he could see that she had gray hair around the temples and guessed her to be around forty to forty-five years of age. He grinned as he moved on down the walkway in the opposite direction. She obviously was a "fancy" and had a mean temper. "Nothing worse than an ill-tempered woman," he said derisively.

Rocking by the fire, he mused over the affairs of the day. *I never did get the lady's name*, he remembered. *Doesn't matter, I probably will never see her again anyway.* He smiled as he remembered her fireworks. *Spunky. Not bad-lookin' either. Had quite the gait too*, he thought.

He grabbed his pipe from the end table and lit it. The sweet essence filled the room. The fire warmed his leg and felt good after all the commotion in town. He was tired. Maybe tonight he could finally get into bed. His back was sore from all the nights in the rocker. He snuffed out his pipe and placed it on the table, then made his way to the bedroom. He undressed and slipped between the sheets. He turned on his side and closed his eyes.

Pearly was there again tonight. He opened his eyes. *I can't keep dreaming about her. It used to bring me comfort, but now I wish I could sleep without those dreams*, he thought. At least his nightmares from the war had been replaced by her. That was progress, but maybe it was just time to move on. He punched his pillow, lay down his head, and drifted off to a dreamless sleep.

CHAPTER 12

R aff stared at the piles of paperwork again. Seemed like several years' worth of bills. He picked one up from the Farm and Feed store. Big red stamp that said *Overdue*. The next one was decorated with the same red stamp. And the next. He picked up the pile and shuffled through them. Red was everywhere. With his elbows on the table, he bowed and put his head in his hands. With a heavy sigh, he lifted his head and raked his hand through his hair. He rubbed the back of his neck. He didn't understand. On the one hand, there were all these overdue bills; and on the other hand, there were all these first edition books. It didn't take a genius to see the incongruencies here. Especially with both the bills and the books in the same room.

Maybe Dad was a schizophrenic, like in *Jekyll and Hyde. Wonder if he has that book up there too.* He pondered.

Why didn't he just sell some books to pay off his debts? It seemed like such a logical step to take. Why didn't he? Raff pinched his nose and closed his eyes.

He started to pull out the drawers to see what else he could find. Stapler, staples, paper clips, Scotch tape—the usual office stuff. He pulled on one drawer, and it seemed to be stuck. He pulled again, and then looked underneath the drawer and found an envelope. *What now, Dad?* he wondered. He pulled it out and opened the envelope. A skeleton key dropped out. No written note as to what it was for, what it might unlock.

He shook his head. "Boy, Alice in Wonderland has nothing on me. It's like I fell into an alternate universe or something," he muttered. "Curiouser and curiouser," he puzzled. He wondered what secrets this key held. Where to start? "How do I unravel this weird mystery?" he whispered. He slammed his fist on the table. Everything was so complicated. *When had Dad gotten so complex? He seemed like a pretty simple guy. Almost a one-track mind, or so it seemed.*

"Did Mom know about any of this stuff, and if so, why hadn't she straightened him out?" So many puzzle pieces, and no way to put them together. He needed help, but who could he trust? Most people would take the books and run. No, he had to find someone he could trust without reservation. But who? His lawyer? Dad never had friends. He needed someone who could lead him to other people for some much-needed answers.

Maybe it was time to take a walk around the farm. Maybe find some hiding places—like the stables. He could start there. He walked into the living room; put on his coat, boots, and scarf; and walked out the door. A blast of frigid air attacked his lungs. "Wow! I forgot how cold it could get here." He coughed. *On second thought, seems like a good day to read in front of the fire.*

He turned around, opened the door, walked inside, and quickly closed it. Turning toward the peg on the wall, he took off his outerwear. He added more wood to the fire and then stood there until his backside was warm, then turned to the front. He rubbed his hands together, reminding himself that he needed to find a good warm pair of gloves and maybe a stocking cap. He walked over to his chair and sat down. Shaking his head, he decided to put it all out of his mind for a while. He was tired. He leaned back in the chair and rested his head. The warmth from the fire seemed to soothe his weary spirit. He drifted off to sleep.

Maddie was sitting beside Raff on the settee, engaged in witty conversation. The laughter that rang from her lips seemed as sweet as ice cream. Those perfect lips. He put his arm around her and drew her into him. She slid closer. He lifted her chin and moved slowly

toward her lips. He could feel her warm breath on his face. He wondered if she could hear his heartbeat as it hammered loudly. He traced
her chin with his fingers, then pulled a stray curl from her eyes. So
close to her lips. He brushed them lightly…and woke up.

"Oh no! I don't want to wake up now." He was wishing with
everything in him it wasn't a dream. He wanted to know what it felt
like to kiss her long and passionately. He yearned for that opportunity. What a disappointment!

"Well, it wasn't a complete loss," he reasoned. "I did get to kiss
her." Oh, how he enjoyed her company. But would she even want
to see him again after the other night? What a coward he had been.
He should have had the guts to tell her and get it over with. Then
he would know for sure whether he would lose her forever, or if he
would have another opportunity. *She'll probably never want to see me
again. Maybe I don't even have a ghost of a chance.* Ghosts! He picked
up Scrooge and began reading.

> Oh! But he was a tight-fisted hand at the
> grindstone, Scrooge! A squeezing, wrenching,
> clutching, covetous old sinner!

"Wow! He didn't hold back on his description of him at all."
He grinned. *This guy was quite the character, one that everyone wanted
to stay away from, for good reason. I may be a lot of things, but this guy
takes the cake,* he thought. The further he got into the book, the more
fascinated he became. It seemed like he had no redeeming values at
all.

Raff's eyes were getting heavy. Putting the book back on the
table, he walked into the bedroom. Yawning, he undressed, pulled
down the covers, and climbed into bed, falling asleep as soon as his
head hit the pillow.

CHAPTER 13

U pon arriving home, Kathleen busied herself with putting away the goods she bought from the General Store. She put the cheese, lettuce, and butter into the fridge. Walking into the bedroom, she took her new undergarments out of the package and placed them in her top drawer. Funny how new undergarments make a woman feel more confident. *Good thing they didn't fall out when that brute ran into me.* Just thinking about that made her cheeks blush.

The man simply had no manners at all! Yet she couldn't stop thinking about him. There was just something about the way his eyes twinkled when he bowed and apologized. She got an inkling that there was a smile that could emerge at any second, but when she took a closer look, there was none. Still…

Kathleen's home, while not a palace, was an estate of affluence and quite lovely. Her father, who had millions worth of stock in a popular car company, had left it to her in his will along with all the staff that he employed and paid quite handsomely. It was not ostentatious, but certainly showed tremendous prosperity and good taste. Everything was perfectly done. From the fashionable draperies to the Persian rugs that seemed to grace each room. The house was not new construction, but that was part of its appeal. Built at the turn of the century, it had columns on each side of the front porch. There were one hundred acres of gardens that were maintained so that there were flowers blooming every season of the year—except winter. Course, the greenhouses took care of the winter flowers. They hothoused poinsettias to sell for the Christmas season and were very successful.

She hadn't grown up in Colorado, so the lack of goods and services irritated her. It wasn't at all like living in New York. But she did love the land out west and was quite comfortable in her home. If necessary, she could order her clothing from the east coast instead of trying to make do. She was never very good at "making do." She wanted what she wanted and had the means to get it. So why shouldn't she?

She loved gift giving. During Christmas, she always made certain that all the children in the neighborhood received at least one gift to put under the tree. She ordered everything from a toy store in San Francisco, knowing they had the finest quality and the largest inventory of any store on the west coast. She also made sure that each business in town had a poinsettia to help decorate for Christmas. While semi-altruistic, it was also free advertising for their own poinsettia farm. They shipped the plants all over North America and really could have lived on that income alone.

White Willow River ran on the far side of her property. She loved walking back there and listening to the water flowing. There was such a peaceful quality to it. It gave her space to think and breathe in the cool, crisp air in the winter and warm sunshine in the summer. There were times when it became a danger in the spring with the swift water from the mountain runoff, but most of the time, even sheep could have taken water from there. Some of the trees hung over the river and provided shade while drinking in that cold, sweet, pure liquid.

It was several months ago when she met George Mayfield. It wasn't exactly the way most people were introduced, but it was very timely. It was late spring, and the sunshine was warm and inviting. Blueberries grew wild on the backside of the property, and she decided to get some air and bring Hettie some berries for jam. She took a basket from the pantry and headed off to the fields. It was something she looked forward to every year. This spring, they had more rain than usual, so the river ran high and rapid.

She wore her favorite high-heeled boots—never fit for hiking, but they looked incredible! She was always dressed to the nines. Reaching for a handful of berries, she lost her footing. She attempted to grab onto something, anything, that could keep her from falling all the way down, but to no avail. She tumbled down the steep hill directly into the water. She screamed as she fell, until the cold blast of the water reached her body and took her breath away. She hung on to a limb from a tree that had fallen across the river and swallowed more than her share of the swirling white. She tried to pull herself up onto the tree, but the water kept pulling her back. Marveling at the water's power, she hung on with all her might, but her fingers kept slipping. The water was frigid, and she knew if the rapids didn't get her, the temperature of the water would.

She kept screaming. Knowing she was too far from the house for anyone to hear, and her strength was waning, she prayed that the Lord would help her—give her the strength she needed to climb up onto that tree. With each attempt, weakness gripped her, and she knew her time for rescue was fleeting.

CHAPTER 14

May 1950

George had decided just last night that tomorrow was the day he would try out his new rod and reel. He loved fishing and hadn't done it in years. He wasn't exactly sure why that was, but tomorrow was his day. He went to bed with excitement he hadn't felt since long before Raff left home. He knew it was kind of silly to be so enthused, but there were few pleasures he'd allowed himself to enjoy for a while, and he thought he had earned it. Besides, the peace and quiet would give him time to think while enjoying a piece of the outdoors he hadn't experienced in a long time. The sunshine and fresh air in new surroundings would be good for his soul. Communing with nature and with God was always beneficial.

He rose earlier than usual. He didn't even have to set the alarm, because he was up and dressed long before dawn. He poured himself a hot cup of coffee, black, and fried two eggs. He didn't know how long he would be gone, so he quickly made himself a ham sandwich with mayo and lettuce. He grabbed a banana and threw both of them in a bag. He looked for his thermos and found it on the top shelf behind a blue pitcher and filled it with coffee. Placing it with the other items, he grabbed the bag along with his rod and a fishing box full of homemade flies, extra fishing wire, and knives. With a twinkle in his eyes and a broad smile on his lips, he set out walking toward the river where the water was still flowing but had no rapids.

When he found the right spot, he sat down, opened his box, chose the perfect fly, and baited his hook. He let down his line and sat down. The sunrise was spectacular and provided the perfect setting. He leaned back and closed his eyes as the sunshine rose in the sky and warmed his face.

"Ah, nothing could be better than this," he breathed. *Now this is the life*, he thought as he took in his surroundings. Such peace he hadn't felt in a long time.

He thought he heard a sound that was contrary to the scene in front of him. No, he must be imagining it. He listened closer. The birds all around him were singing and communicating with one another, and he loved their music and interaction.

Wait! There it was again. What was that? It was faint, but it sounded like a human scream. He threw his rod and reel down on the bank, high enough so the river wouldn't have its way with it, and tried to make out from which direction the sound came.

There it was again. It came from upstream. He climbed the bank and ran as fast as he could. Course, being forty-eight and out of shape, his fast wasn't all that fast. He sensed the urgency in the voice and knew whoever it was, it sounded like they needed help several minutes ago. He might already be too late. He lumbered around the corner and saw her. She was all the way down the hill, soaked to the skin, and looking quite weak. He hurried down the hill, careful not to fall. He needed his wits about him. She looked too far out for him to try to get into the river to help her, so he had to quickly find another way. He looked around and saw a loose branch. Picking it up on the way down the hill, he called to her.

"Hey, I'm here! Are you okay?"

She looked frightened and weary. He knew he needed to move quickly, or she wasn't going to make it.

"Listen! Can you take hold of this branch so I can pull you in," he yelled, trying to be heard over the roar of the water.

Her head sank under the water, and George started to panic. *I've got to get her out of the water, now!*

He knew she was too far gone for the branch idea. Any second now, she would let go, and he'd never be able to catch her. He threw the branch away and made his way into the water. The white water swirled around him. It got deeper, and he attempted to get something solid underneath him so they both didn't get swept away.

He was still too far away from her. He stepped down farther as the water came up around his waist. It was freezing, but the adrenaline racing through him seemed to keep him warm enough. One more step, and he could reach her. He slipped, and he grabbed a small branch close by to steady himself. Her head emerged for just a second and was under the water again. One hand fell to the water just as he reached and was able to catch it. He started to slip again when he prayed, "God, help me!"

He started to pull her toward him, and her head bobbed up again. He quickly reached for her other hand, grabbed it, and yelled for her to hang on. She nodded, indicating she would try.

She wrapped her hands around his wrists, and he pulled her hard as he backed up to the edge of the river. Tripping over a rock, but determined not to let her go, they both went under, but then he was able to ground himself again, and slowly he pulled her until they reached the bank. He placed her on the ground. He fell on his knees beside her and tried to see if she was okay, other than being waterlogged and exhausted.

It was obvious that she was spent, but she wouldn't open her eyes. He hoped that was just exhaustion, but he was wary. Should he leave her and go for help? He started to lightly slap her face, to bring her to. She was breathing. That he knew for sure. But anything beyond that, he was uncertain.

"Ma'am, ma'am. Please wake up! Ma'am," he shouted.

Her eyes started moving, and finally her eyelashes started shifting upward.

"Ma'am, can you hear me?" he asked.

She moved her hand to his, too tired for words. He instinctively understood the soundless reply. He smiled down to her. "You're okay then!" he said, bursting with joy. "Hallelujah! Thank you, God," he rejoiced, thankfully and gleefully. It was a few minutes before she was able to speak.

"Thank you," she whispered. "I... I...couldn't hold on for one more second. I was ready to go to Jesus," she said tearfully. "I guess he's not finished with me yet," she said, closing her eyes again.

George told her to rest, and he would try to find something with which to cover her. He made his way up the hill and saw the estate in the distance. He wished he were in better shape so he could run to the house. He felt he just wasn't going fast enough. He kept moving until he reached the front steps. Knocking on the door and feeling like it was taking way too long for the door to open, he nervously moved around while fisting and unfisting his hands.

The door opened, and the words tumbled out of his mouth all jumbled. The lady told him to slow down so she could understand. He quickly explained that there was a lady who fell in the river. He got her out, but she needed a blanket and help getting her home—wherever that was.

Hettie Blackstone ran upstairs and quickly retrieved a wool blanket. She stepped lightly down the stairs and gave him the blanket, adding she would send some men to help him. Taking hold of the blanket, he quickly explained exactly where she was and turned to leave. He made his way through the fields again, totally out of breath. He had to stop for a few seconds to catch his breath, then continued. He turned around and saw two men heading for him, running at a pretty fast clip. Relieved, he kept on. The hill was right in front of him, and he finally reached the crest. He took a deep breath and made his way down the hill.

She was still lying down, which concerned him, but he knelt and put the blanket around her, essentially tucking her in. She was shaking wildly. He lay down and pulled her body close to his. He needed to warm her body, quickly. Her teeth were chattering. The two young men came roaring down the hill and bent down to pick her up. George saw recognition in their eyes. They knew her.

The men looked at each other. "That's Miss Kathleen," they said together.

Reaching down, they wrapped the blanket around her, and one of them picked her up and slung her over his shoulder and started jogging to the estate, with the other close by.

George just hoped she would be all right. He started to walk after them, but he suddenly started shaking and fell to the ground. He wasn't sure what was wrong, but he did know he desperately needed rest. He was freezing. He needed to get home, but first he needed to be certain Miss Kathleen, as they called her, was going to be okay.

The adrenaline was gone. He couldn't go one more step. George wanted nothing more than to sleep, but how was he going to find out about Kathleen? His eyes closed.

He heard something in the distance. He couldn't wrap his head around what was making the sound. Was that someone talking? He felt foggy, sluggish. He tried to move, but nothing would. He tried to open his eyes, but they would not obey his command. Someone was talking, but who? His eyes slowly opened but were hazy. He tried to focus but couldn't. His mind started to clear and heard men speaking to him but wasn't sure what they were saying.

"Sir, sir…can you hear me?" he said, alarm ringing in his voice.

George tried to think. Where was he, and who was talking to him? He did have the presence of mind to nod at them. He could hear them now.

He felt a much-appreciated warmth cover his body. Someone wrapped a blanket around him and flung him over his shoulder and started jogging. At this point, he really didn't care, if he could finally sleep and feel warm again. He closed his eyes. He felt safe and tired—mostly tired.

When he awoke, his eyes darted around the room. He didn't recognize anything. He thought it was a bedroom, but it was bigger than any bedroom he'd ever seen. Was it a hotel? No, it looked like a home, but certainly not like anyone's he knew. He started to get up, and his head spun. He lay back down. Wherever he was, he would be staying, at least until his head stopped spinning. His eyes closed again, and he slept peacefully.

CHAPTER 15

December 1950

Raff had intended to get back into the office and work. But on what? All he had was a stack of overdue bills, a bookcase full of expensive books, and a skeleton key that opened what? He shook his head. All he had were questions with no answers. Needing a break from all things that had to do with his father, he talked himself into another round with Scrooge.

He was enjoying this book except for one thing; it made him think about his own life. He was never one for introspection, but in this case, he felt that it was going to happen whether he wanted it to or not. The first ghost, the Ghost of Christmas Past, revealed Scrooge's bad decisions and what they had done to him. With that he could identify.

His thoughts strayed toward Maddie. Why did he always end up there? He rehearsed their last conversation and was ashamed. He really wanted to see her again. It had only been two days since he'd seen her, but it felt like a month. The truth was that no matter how messed up his life was, Maddie was the one person upon whom he could count. She challenged him to be a better person. And that was the point. He wasn't a better person. She deserved a better man. One who could offer her more than a man with a life that was damaged—broken. His father continually told him that he would never amount to anything, that he was worthless. Even on the things he loved doing.

Working with wood was what he enjoyed the most. He built the tree house in which he and Maddie had spent so much time. He found it brought him so much pleasure and joy. After that, he built an oak table and chairs, complete with some hand carving in the center, built a china cabinet out of cherry that stunned the neighborhood, and a chest of drawers from pine. Many told him to sell the pieces; they were convinced he could make enough money to make it worth his while. He was that good. He was filled with pride, but it was short-lived.

His father never saw the value in it. Desperately, Raff tried to explain to his father how building things made him feel alive and brought him joy. But when the wood was gone, his dad told him he couldn't buy more; besides, he needed to get serious about going to college instead of playing around with wood. That was worthless and so was he. He needed to make something of himself. Be somebody of whom he could be proud. In the end, he lived down to his father's expectations, and his woodworking career was over—permanently!

He gave the furniture away to a family in need. Their house had burned to the ground and had lost everything. The officials suspected arson but couldn't prove it. They were renting now, and Raff felt good handing his work over to them. At least someone could benefit from it.

The other occupation that he enjoyed was that of a mechanic. He fixed everything he could get his hands on. Cars, transistor radios, appliances, anything and everything. That's where he made his living, but mostly from cars. He'd worked in a shop in Denver with the owner the five years he was gone. With almost any work he did with his hands, he excelled.

School, however, was not one of them. He was smart enough, but the teachers didn't think he was engaged or listening. But he was, and he learned. The problem was, he really hadn't cared. He didn't take it seriously, and that was the thing his teachers and his dad never understood.

Even though he wasn't finished with Scrooge, he couldn't help searching himself.

How does one correct his mistakes? "If I can't ever forgive my dad, how can I expect anyone to forgive me? Can I ever move on? I've had all kinds of time to do that, and yet I haven't. What I've done was despicable!" he almost spat the words.

I can't tell her. She will hate me and will never want to see me again. Maybe even be repulsed by me—which would be worse. I don't think I could live with that. His thoughts seemed to be coming from everywhere at one time.

"God help me, I couldn't live with that. God? Where did that come from? I've never thought of him before, at least not for help, but only to deny his existence or his interest and love for people," he deliberated.

How can he soothe Maddie's heartache and hurt he'd caused? *If only I had stayed that night and taken her in my arms. Oh, I wanted to, but then the temptation to kiss her would have been too great. Those lips. Those beautiful bow-shaped lips that I have come to desire.* "Maybe I could just talk to her without getting into the hard stuff. Right. How would that work? How would avoiding it make her feel better?" he felt so confused. He put his head in his hands. "I can't think anymore."

He grabbed Scrooge again. Scrooge was one unfeeling, greedy grouch. Selfish to the core. Mean and cantankerous. That wasn't part of the book. Those were his thoughts about him. "I was never that bad, was I?" he questioned his own character. Then he wondered if there were layers of mistakes and sins. Was one worse than another?

Reading about the Ghost of Christmas Past made him realize that all the wrong decisions Scrooge had made had led him to the person he'd become—bitter and angry. Hmm. That sort of sounded familiar.

Am I bitter and angry? he asked, testing himself.

It didn't take him long to answer that question. *Yes, and I can add unforgiving to that list as well.* He felt like he was looking into a mirror and didn't like what he'd seen. Facing the truth head-on, he had to admit that he was no better than Scrooge. Pretty much all the rotten qualities, if you wanted to call them that, Scrooge had, Raff had too. He had allowed bitterness, anger, and unforgiveness to enter his heart and was poisoning him. They had been his companions for years, and they were destroying his life. "Forgiveness. But how do I forgive my father? He hurt me for years, repeatedly."

"How, God, how?" he cried out.

His knees fell to the floor, and tears streamed down his cheeks.

"God, I know I need to forgive, but I can't do it. If you're real and you do love me, please help me forgive my father. I have been so wrong about everything. I feel so broken. Please heal me and put the pieces back together. Take all the regret, pain, and the terrible things that I've done and make me different. I'm so tired of fighting you and the world. I give myself to you. I don't want to live like this anymore." He stayed on his knees. "I ask you to please forgive me, God."

You are forgiven, my son.

He heard a voice. A whisper, really. He looked around, but there was no one there.

He couldn't move. He could barely breathe. Was...was that the voice...of God?

Suddenly, he felt odd. What was that feeling? It took him a few seconds. Peace. It was peace. Joy. Two emotions he hadn't felt in a very long time. It was miraculous. A smile crossed his face as he got to his feet. He felt lighter somehow, like a burden had been lifted off his shoulders. What was weird was that even his face seemed to relax. He walked to a mirror and studied his face. He could have sworn that some of his small lines and wrinkles were gone. Course, at twenty-five, he didn't have that many to begin with. *That's ridiculous,* he thought. And something else. There seemed to be a glow... His eyes had a sparkle he hadn't seen before. "That's impossible. I'm just imagining it."

This new peace felt great! "So, what's next? What do I do now?" he asked, ready to move on in this newfound joy he was experiencing. *I need to talk to someone that knows a lot more about God than I do,* he thought. *"But who? Maddie."*

CHAPTER 16

May 1950

Kathleen awoke in her bedroom and didn't remember going to bed. In fact, the last thing she remembered was leaving the house and going to the fields to pick wild blueberries. But for the life of her, she couldn't remember anything else. She sat up on her elbows and realized how much her arms ached. She searched her memory to try to figure out what she had done that would result in the extreme soreness in her arms and hands. She lay back down and closed her eyes, hoping some recollection would come to her. Taking stock of her body, she realized that it wasn't just her arms and hands that hurt, her whole body hurt. She looked closer and saw scratches and small cuts and bruises all over her body. Her head started throbbing. *What on earth…?*

She called Hettie to come to her room. Within a few seconds, she was by her bedside.

"You called, honey?" she asked.

"Yes, Hettie, I did. Can you please tell me what happened? I'm bruised and battered and sore everywhere."

"Ya don't remember, huh?"

"I think if I'd remembered, I wouldn't have asked, would I?" she replied impatiently.

"No, s'pose not."

She sat on the bed and gently stroked her hair.

"Sweetheart, ya fell down a hill and landed in the river, where ya hung on for goodness knows how long before ya got rescued. Ya purt' near drowned. Ya only had a couple more seconds before them rapids would've taken ya clean down that river. The good Lord was sure watchin' over ya. Yes, sir, he surely was," she explained. "By the way," she continued, "ya need to throw them boots in the river! Them are useless and, in your case, downright dangerous! Purtty might work well in New York City, honey, but not here. You need to get ya some real boots," she added.

Hettie had been the housekeeper for the Brennan family for thirty years. Her skin was a warm light, brown tone, and her hair, mostly gray now, was still beautiful. The smile she wore was bigger than the whole outdoors. She was a trusted friend and confidante. She raised Kathleen along with her own daughter, Jessie. The girls were the same age and were best friends until they grew up. Jessie got married and moved away. Kathleen was crushed, but happy for her. Jessie always called her Kathy, but she preferred Kathleen, a fact she had told her many times. She never listened to her and called her Kathy anyway. It became a term of endearment—like a nickname of sorts. But she was the only one that ever got away with it.

The memories started flooding back like the rapids on the river. She winced as she recalled the details. *No wonder I hurt everywhere,* she thought.

"Now honey, ya jes' lay yourself right back down, and I'll bring ya some scrambled eggs and bacon jes' like ya like 'em," she said, like the caretaker she had always been.

"Just how long have I been asleep, Hettie?"

"Jes' a couple days s'all. Now, ya lie back here, and I'll fetch ya some breakfast right away."

"I'm not really hungry, Hettie," she said as she tried to get up. She groaned. Obviously, she was in no shape to go anywhere.

"Doc said ya be all right in a few days. Till then ya s'posed to rest. I'll bring ya some aspirin that he left for ya. That'll help with them bumps and bruises painin' ya. I'll be back in two shakes of a lamb's tail. Now no arguin'. Ya need some food to get back your strength. I'll bring up a tray for ya," she said as she hurried out of the room, down the stairs, and into the kitchen.

Kathleen sighed. *A few days? I've got things to do,* she thought, *although I can't think of anything pressing right now.* Lying back down, her mind wandered. *Who rescued me?* She wondered. *Did Hettie say?* She wasn't sure. She remembered thinking she was going to die and was ready to meet her mother and Jesus. She didn't wish to die, but if death came, she was ready for it.

Hettie breezed back in with the tray filled with scrambled eggs, bacon, toast, and coffee. Kathleen looked the tray over and said she would try to eat. Hettie fluffed up her pillows so she could sit up. She gently lifted her so she could rest against them. Making sure she was well situated, she lay the tray across her lap. Kathleen winced as she set it down. Did everything have to hurt quite so much? Hettie headed for the door advising her to eat and explaining that she would be back up to take the tray and bring her some aspirin and water. With that, she took her leave.

Kathleen took a few bites then circled the plate with her fork. She couldn't eat. She was, however, ready for those aspirin. She took a few sips of coffee and a bite of toast. Her arms screamed as she tried to lift the tray. She tried again and grunted as she lifted it high enough to push it onto the side table. That was it. All the energy she could muster. She rested her head on the pillows and drifted off.

CHAPTER 17

December 1950

Maddie opened the door to see Raff standing there. She searched his face and then lowered her head.

"What are you doing here, Raff? You made it perfectly clear you didn't want to have anything to do with me a few days ago. So, why don't you just leave me alone." Her face filled with grief.

His heart broke for her.

"Maddie, please, let me in. I need to talk to you. Please," he pleaded.

She sighed. "Fine." She turned away and sat down on the sofa.

She expected him to walk over to the chair where he usually sat, but instead, he sat with her on the couch.

Looking surprised, she scooted over to her side next to the arm. He studied her face.

"Maddie, I'm so sorry I did that to you. I really didn't mean to hurt you. But I need to tell you so many things, and I hope you are willing to listen. It won't be easy for me. I'm so afraid that after I tell you about all the terrible things I've done, you won't want to see me ever again." His eyes drifted down to his feet in regret.

"Raff, there's nothing you can tell me that will change my opinion of you, but you don't have to tell me anything. I know you had a life away from the farm, but I don't need to know about it. It's okay," she argued.

"You don't understand. I have to tell you. Maddie, you're the only friend I have. I know I am risking your friendship by telling you this, but I owe it to you to tell you everything. I only ask one thing."

"What's that?"

"That you please don't interrupt me until I'm finished. Otherwise, I'm not sure I can go through with it."

She nodded. "Okay, I promise."

He let out a hefty breath.

"I left home because I couldn't be around my dad one more minute. The last straw was when he sold Sport. He was the one thing that made me feel good. I hated him for that," he said, grimacing. He let out another big breath and continued. He looked in her eyes.

"I know there are so many ways I could have handled that, but I chose that one. Just a long list of bad choices I've made in my life. I should have told you I was leaving. Well, I shouldn't have left at all, but I did. I should have told my parents. All I could think about was getting as far away from my father as I could. I didn't think about how it would affect everyone else. It was selfish and cruel, and I'm so sorry." Sadness gripped his heart.

Maddie could see how troubled he was, and her heart went out to him, wishing she could take way his pain.

"It gets worse," he whispered.

"Go on." She nodded. "I'm listening."

"Okay," he said as he took a deep breath and blew it out. "After I left, I tried to find happiness anyplace I could. I began drinking and, on several occasions, even blacked out. I woke up in bed with someone I didn't know more times than I could count." He knew this was hurting her, but he had to get through this. It might be the last time he ever saw her. He continued.

"Instead of finding happiness, I just felt empty and depressed. The more I drank, the more I hated myself and took it out on everyone around me. As it turned out, they didn't really care about me anyway, and if I were to be honest, I didn't even know them. They were just drinking buddies and women I didn't love or care about. I just used them." His eyes filled with tears.

"Oh, Raff," she said softly. She tried to take his hand, and he pulled it out.

"Don't try to be nice to me. Not now. I'll never get through this. Besides," he smiled weakly, "you promised not to interrupt."

She smiled. "I did, I'm sorry," she whispered.

"I didn't know where I was going and never tried to tell anyone where to get in touch with me. I couldn't deal with the way I was living my life and certainly couldn't tell anyone about it. I was so ashamed, but there wasn't anything else to fill that void I was feeling.

"Then Abigail Jenkins walked into my life. We went out to a restaurant and had dinner. I drank several drinks and took her home. I tried to...well, you know. She smacked me a good one right across my face!"

He smiled as he recalled the look on her face. "That, I was not expecting. Not that I didn't deserve it, you understand. I didn't know that she had seen me around before. She knew my reputation. She went out with me anyway. She had her reasons, and they were good ones.

"Anyway, she sat me down and spoke the truth. First time I'd listened to the truth in a long time. She told me that if I kept going down the path I was currently on, it would kill me. It felt like another slap in the face. That there was no way I would experience happiness running from everything that was good. Women and alcohol were destroying me. That was a gut punch. A great big dose of reality from a tiny sweet woman. She was small, but mighty. She was willing to be my friend, but only if I gave up all the stuff that had held me hostage. What I was doing was only running away from old hurts and disappointments.

"That day, things changed. I gave up the destructive lifestyle. But the problem was that I held on to the bitterness and anger that was raging in my heart. I couldn't forgive my father, and I hated myself for what I did to other people. I used them, Maddie." He sniffed, holding back tears.

CHAPTER 18

May 1950

George awakened again and sat up. The dizziness was gone. That was good news. He still had no idea where he was, but his memory had returned. His thoughts turned to Kathleen and wondered how she was doing and how to get in touch with her. He threw the covers off and realized he was undressed for bed and wondered how that happened. He didn't remember doing that. He looked around the room and saw his clothes on the chair in the corner, cleaned and pressed. *Wow! Such service*, he thought.

He walked over to the chair and dressed. He sighed as he sat down. His energy was already waning. "Well, buck up, old man, you've got to get out of here and find Kathleen."

He put on his shoes and socks and sauntered over to the door. Opening it, he saw the wrought iron curved stairway. Between the railings was a floral pattern with leaves and long stems. It was beautiful, and the steps were made from cherrywood, wide at the bottom and narrowing going up...but there was something familiar about them. He couldn't quite put his finger on exactly why that was.

He walked down the stairs and peeked into the living room. The dizziness returned. He grabbed the staircase and leaned against it. *Who are these people?* he wondered. *This house is something else.* Standing up and walking toward the hall, he ran into Mrs. Blackstone.

"Oh, so ya feelin' better, sir?" she asked.

"Yes, ma'am, thank you." A flash of recognition swept over his face. "Wait! You're the one who answered the door when I was asking for help for the woman that fell in the river, right?"

"Yep, that's right. And thanks to ya, 'cept for some bumps and bruises, Miss Kathleen be right as rain in a couple days or so. We don't know how to thank ya," she said with the broadest smile he had ever seen.

"You don't need to thank me. I'm just so relieved she'll be all right."

"Would you mind tellin' me your name, sir?" she asked.

"Not at all. George Mayfield, at your service, ma'am." He nodded his head.

"Well, ain't you something, Mr. Mayfield. Glad to make your acquaintance, sir." She chuckled.

"Thank you, ma'am. Likewise, I'm sure.

Well, I need to take my leave. Thank you so much for taking care of me. That was mighty kind of you. I promise, I will repay you."

"No need, sir. Happy to do it. Good patient. Slept the whole time." She laughed.

"Well, doesn't sound very hospitable of me." He chuckled. "Would you be so kind as to tell Miss Kathleen how glad I am that she's okay? I was so afraid I wasn't going to be able to get to her in time."

"I surely will, sir. She's mighty grateful to ya. We all are."

"Well, I must be going," he said as he strode toward the door. "Thank you, again."

She beat him to the door, opened it, and bid him goodbye.

CHAPTER 19

December 1950

Looking around the cabin, Franklin remembered again the Christmas decorations that Pearly put up right after Thanksgiving. He told her several times that if he cut down the tree too early, they'd have to cut down another halfway through the season. He chuckled as he remembered how she laughed at that. She figured that was okay because there were so many out there from which to choose. Never deterred her one bit. He still cut it down early, and she would decorate it early. He had to admit to himself that he loved the decorations even though he never told her that. Why hadn't he? Was he afraid she wouldn't think him manly enough? She always said he was mushy inside. *Enough of this*, he thought. *It's time to move on.*

The weather had warmed a little, so he decided to get some fresh air. He put on his hat and coat, opened the door, and walked through, closing the door behind him. He breathed in the fresh air and limped down the stairs. Every time the weather changed, he could feel it in his leg.

With the warmer temperatures, it wouldn't be too long before the snow melted. Couldn't be too soon to suit him. Even though it was still December, he longed for spring. These winters could get so long and depressing. He sighed as he walked toward the barn. He stepped over a patch of ice just when Barney walked under his feet, unseen, and Franklin went sprawling to the ground. His bad leg landed underneath him. He yelled a few curse words, and the startled cat ran off. Trying to move from the ground with nothing to hang onto was sometimes difficult. His head hung down and he sighed. Taking in a deep breath, he moved his leg. It wasn't moving easily. He moved his good leg, and with his hands around the other leg, he positioned it so both legs were flat to the ground. He was a strong and proud man, but this made him feel helpless and weak. He twisted from the waist and placed his hands on the ground. Pushing up with his arm strength, he stood on his good leg, and his other leg followed. That was it. He was going inside. He chopped some wood for the fire and piled it into his arms. He winced as he limped up the stairs and carefully opened the door and dropped the wood on the floor. The fire was still in good shape for a while, so he walked to the bedroom to get some dry clothes on. After changing, he walked to the fire, bent over, and stoked the fire. Plopping into the chair, he lit his pipe and raked his hand through his hair.

It was a habit he'd had from his youth, back when he'd had curly locks. That was one of the things that Pearly loved about him. When younger, she would sit on his lap and run her fingers through his hair. She'd stop and shyly pull his head down so she could kiss him. He smiled and shook his head. She never really outgrew that shyness. He loved that about her. It gave her an innocence that she kept all those years.

He laid his head back against the chair and rocked, allowing his memories to wash over him like a spring rain. He opened his eyes not wanting to drop his pipe again, snuffed it out, and placed it on the table. He closed his eyes and began to drift.

Kathleen stepped out from the General Store and walked toward him. He took a longer look at her than he should have, but just couldn't look away. She had deep brown eyes that seemed to reflect off the sun. She was petite, but certainly had a shapely figure, and knew how to modestly emphasize it. She had been trained, probably boarding school or tutors. With a straight spine, she walked with a confidence that few women around here possessed. Her auburn hair, which had been curled in the latest fashion, including a ridiculous-looking hat, was beautiful in the sunlight. Even the silver around her temples only served to make her more attractive. He wondered what her hair felt like and found himself wanting to rake his fingers through it. He could tell by some of the whiffs of hair on her cheeks, before the salon fashioned it, was naturally tiny, tight curls. So very attractive. He wondered why she would want to change that.

The cat jumped up on the porch, and he awoke with a start. He had been dreaming again, but this time it wasn't about the war or Pearly. It was about Kathleen. It gave him goose bumps, and he dismissed them along with the possibility that a woman like Kathleen would ever have anything to do with a cripple like him.

He sighed as he stood up, added wood to the fire, turned out the lights and went to bed. Even though the day hadn't been long, he felt like it had. His leg ached from the fall, but he thought maybe a good night's sleep in his bed would help that. He had to be more careful. He was glad there was no one around to see him fall. He switched off the light and walked to the bedroom, looking forward to his bed and laying his head on his pillow.

CHAPTER 20

October 1950

George clutched his chest as a pain struck him like lightning. He'd had a few now and again, but lately they seemed to be getting stronger. The new medication he was taking wasn't working, or maybe he was just feeling more stressed. He sat in his chair while the pain settled down and finally left. Maybe he'd read the prescription wrong and wasn't taking enough.

After his heart settled, his thoughts turned to Olivia. He regretted that he never really knew how to love her, let alone Raff. He wished he could turn back the clock and start that part of his life over. He would have changed so many things. He pushed everyone away, even Liv.

She had taken care of the books for the farm, paying bills, keeping track of the bank accounts and services. But everything changed when she was diagnosed with cancer. He didn't want to burden her with all that work.

Since George was never good with numbers, and Liv could no longer take care of that, he hired a very well-recommended lawyer by the name of Lucas Sprat. The manager at the bank had said that Lucas was an upstanding man of stellar character, and he had many accounts at the bank of people just like him who needed a little help.

George was so relieved not to have to worry anymore, that he turned everything over to him.

Since Raff left home, George was Liv's only caretaker. He watched as she wasted away into skin and bones. Her excruciating pain and severe nausea and vomiting left her weak and unresponsive. He tried to help her. It hurt so badly to watch her suffer. He even went so far as to pray to God for help; after all, it brought peace to her.

He'd watched her through the years walking to church with her Bible in hand on Sundays and Wednesdays and on any special get-togethers. He thought it was all worthless and wishful thinking. But now, since he knew Liv was not going to survive, his heart ached with the thought of losing her. He cared for her, but he never learned how to express it. He didn't know, maybe he even loved her in his own way.

It wasn't long before he'd buried her in the church cemetery. He always thought that being alone would bring him peace. No one to worry about or to fight with, no one to nag him. Instead, he felt empty, like this house. Alone with his thoughts and rash decisions. Alone with his anger and resentment. Just alone.

He couldn't believe how many people came to the service. He didn't want a big hullabaloo, so he kept the service simple, but the people from church showed him so much kindness and love it was hard to take in. Some of them brought meals to him and even stayed and shared it with him. At first it was awkward, but he soon realized how friendly everyone was and how much they cared for her. Because of her, they cared for him. That began his journey to learning about God.

He was in the attic one day looking for old photos when he came upon Liv's Bible. He'd never looked inside it before. He opened it. Right on the first page, he saw one of many notes she had written.

He began reading. "God's silence does not indicate His lack of interest."

Another: "Where God has expressed His will, He will make a way."

Another: "If I would sit down at the feet of Jesus and rest my head on His knees, He would take care of the rest."

He sat on the chair by the window and read them again. Then he saw a scripture reference for Philippians 4:13. He didn't know what that meant exactly, so he looked further and found a page that had a list of names he assumed meant different books. He found the right book. He flipped through the pages until he found the place.

He read: "I can do all things through him who gives me strength."

And 1 John 2:1–2.

"My dear children, I write this to you so you will not sin. But if anybody does sin, we have one who speaks to the Father in our defense—Jesus Christ, the Righteous One. He is the atoning sacrifice for our sin, and not only for ours but also for the sins of the whole world."

He read the note she'd written there. "Jesus Christ comes to our side and faces God every time we sin."

He immediately thought of Raff and the way he had treated him. His memories flooded back like a tsunami.

Raff had found some old wood that had been piled up in the barn and decided to build something. George had always known he loved working with his hands, but he thought this was a waste of time.

There were all different kinds of wood from cherry to oak and pine. Raff made pieces of furniture. He gave them all to people in need. Even told him to sell them, that he could make a living at it. But George only wanted him to go to college and make something of himself.

He wanted Raff to be a better man than he was. Playing with wood, building tree houses, and playing with that kid from next door—were all a waste of time. It was worthless and so was he. He just couldn't understand why Raff didn't want to further his education. Was it so hard for him to understand? He just wanted the best for him.

He realized now there were so many ways he could have told him that and not had to watch the pain and disappointment in his eyes he knew he had caused.

George wished he could take it all back. He'd seen others make a go of woodworking later and wished Raff would come home so he could tell him he had been wrong. So wrong.

He read the part about his sin again. He had way too many to count. He so wanted to change things but he didn't know how. Did Jesus really care that much? Is it possible he could become the man he should have been for Liv and Raff?

When he remembered Raff's eyes full of anger and resentment, he wished he could've taken all those words back. His father had done the same thing to him. Why hadn't he recognized it earlier?

He took her Bible downstairs and started reading in the Gospel of John. He wasn't certain why he chose that book, but he thought someone had said years ago that John was the place to start reading. He spent hours poring through the Bible, and he felt like something was happening he couldn't understand, but it was a good feeling. By midnight, he closed the book and walked to the bedroom.

As the sun rose, so did he. He picked up the Bible and continued reading. He started writing his questions down and thought maybe Pastor Ryan could answer them for him. As the weeks passed, George kept reading and talking to Pastor Ryan. Spring turned to summer, then fall, then winter. It was at the beautiful Christmas Eve service 1948 when George finally gave his heart to Jesus and became a new man. Oh, how he wished he would have learned all this earlier. It would have changed everything.

Pastor helped him see so many things from his past that brought him to this place. He wanted to see Raff and tell him how sorry he was for all the years he had fought with him and the lack of love, the neglect, and verbal abuse he had inflicted. Maybe someday he would come home, and he could make things right. He prayed that would happen, so many times.

CHAPTER 21

December 1950

Maddie looked at Raff with tears in her eyes. She wanted to take him in her arms and comfort him. She'd never seen him so vulnerable and emotional. He usually had his emotions locked up tight and kept under control. She didn't know how to help him, but wanted to with everything in her. She also knew if she moved or interrupted again, he might not be able to continue. The things he had done were awful, but she understood why. She just wished she could have helped him through that time. No, he never would have let her. He didn't confide intimate details of his life. She didn't know how bad the relationship with his father had gotten. He should have told her.

Raff stared at her. What was she thinking? Were the tears he saw in her eyes because she was through with him? Was this really the last time he would be with her? If he asked her at this point, it could be disastrous. So he continued.

"It wasn't long after that I got word that Mom had died. I don't remember who contacted me or how they found me. They said that she died from cancer.

"Maddie, I wasn't even there to help her through it," he said regretfully. "I should have been there. Once she was gone, there wasn't any reason to come home."

Maddie looked wounded.

"I'm sorry, Maddie, I didn't mean it like that."

She nodded. "I know." It still hurt, but she tried not to show it. "When I got news from dad's lawyer, this Lucas Sprat person, that Dad had died, I knew that there were things I needed to do here. The lawyer said I needed to settle the estate. All I wanted to do was sell the farm and get back to my life. I had no idea what that looked like. No job. No real home. Only one friend. The one that talked sense into me, finally.

"Then I saw you. When I walked away from you the other night, I was so confused and didn't know which way to turn. For the first time, I was faced with my anger, bitterness, and unforgiveness. I wrestled with God. I didn't want to forgive Dad, but I knew I had to. Maddie, last night, I gave my life to God. I forgave my father and asked God to forgive me from all my sin and bitterness."

"I even heard God's voice, at least I think it was his, telling me he had forgiven me. I felt real peace and joy for the very first time."

He looked at Maddie, and tears were streaming down her face; they were streaming down his too. She jumped up and hugged him.

"Oh, Raff. I'm so happy for you. I've been praying for you. I wanted you to know Jesus for years. This is wonderful!"

Raff looked at her with those tears and her face glowing and wanted to kiss her in the worst way, but he knew this wasn't the time. This was the time for purity and a newfound innocence for him. One he wasn't going to mess up.

"Now I need someone to help me learn more about God and what he wants from me. How to pray and how to read the Bible and understand what it's saying. Will you help me do that, Maddie?"

He took his hands and held hers. A shiver starting from her toes ran all the way up her spine.

He studied her.

"Oh, yes, Raff. I would love to. And when the questions come that I can't answer, we can go to Pastor Ryan at church where your mom went. He's a great guy, and I know you'll like him," she said excitedly. "Besides, I go there too, so he knows me."

Still holding hands, Raff suddenly became aware and pulled his hands away. He would have loved to continue that but knew not to.

"How do we start?"

"Well, why don't you start with writing down all your questions. I'll try to answer them. Can't promise you I can, but I'll try," she said sweetly.

He finally admitted to himself that he was in love with her. She didn't reject him. She embraced him. How unexpected and wonderful. He thanked God for her friendship and loyalty. He should have known that she would stick by him because that's the kind of person she'd always been.

On his way home, he thanked God for his forgiveness and the joy and peace it had brought him. He also thanked him for Maddie. For their friendship, but also that maybe it would lead to something more.

CHAPTER 22

Rusty, Miles Stratton's golden retriever, had been with him for years. Sure, Rusty had lost some of his get-up-and-go, but then so had he. Everywhere Miles went, Rusty followed.

Miles had been on his own since he was sixteen. His dad had left just after he was born, so his mom raised him on her own. She was a God-fearing woman who worked from sunup to sundown every day. Not only did she take care of all the domestic things a woman usually did, but she also worked at the café in town for living expenses while Miles was in school.

It seemed a tranquil life until his mother died from pneumonia. Rusty became his whole world. He didn't have any relatives that he knew of; it had just been him and his mom.

Even though he was sixteen, he easily passed for eighteen, so when WWI broke out, he joined the army. His recruiting officer had a soft spot for dogs, so Rusty was allowed to follow Miles into war.

Miles had no skills really, but they started training him to help in the medical field. There were never enough doctors. Miles was a quick learner and smart. He'd listened and watched how things were done and could mimic them. He learned triage. How to bind wounds until the docs could get to them. In essence, getting them prepared for surgery, which was surely the next step. Having to choose which ones to help and which ones were beyond help was the hardest thing about this job. He would sit and talk to them and tell them lies about how they were going to be okay, and he would often stay with them until they passed on. Rusty would also stay with the wounded, and it brought comfort to the men in their final moments.

Being a medical anything was about the last thing he'd ever thought about doing, but now that he was being used that way, he found he liked it. He didn't have the education he needed to take on the more complicated issues, but he was learning new things every day and was loving it. He vowed that when the war was over, he was going to medical school and become a doctor or whatever was as close to that as he could get.

He learned medications and had dispensed morphine to the soldiers in extreme pain. He knew how to set up intravenous lines for saline solution and medicine. But there was another side. One of death. War always brought death and savagery with it. Broken families, dictators who were only out for their own gain, and soldiers who looted homes in order to sell their possessions on the black market. Whoever said war was hell knew what he was talking about. Nothing good about it except the camaraderie between the men who became brothers. Those friendships lasted a lifetime along with the memories, both good and bad. Unfortunately, so many lifetimes were cut short. That was the hardest part.

It had been raining all day, which made trench warfare the most miserable. Suddenly a gun misfired and hit Rusty in the head. There was nothing anyone could do. All the men grieved the loss. He had become the one bright spot in an otherwise dreary and bloody war. It was the hardest on Miles, but there were wounded to attend, and war raged on, never stopping for grief. Still, in the quiet times, of which there were few, his thoughts always turned to Rusty and all that he'd lost. He wasn't just a dog; he was his friend—the only one upon whom he could confide and depend.

Upon returning home after the war, he discovered the funds needed for medical school were unattainable for him. Someone had informed him, however, that the path to a career in pharmaceuticals was a quicker route, and he would still be helping others. Now, years later, he was the town pharmacist at Rodger's Pharmacy. He really wasn't a people person, as they say, but he filled the prescriptions, mixed the compounds, and explained the medications when required. He made a decent living and was content with his life.

But the war had changed him, and he'd become quiet and kept to himself. Most folks didn't understand that and had branded him as strange. The kids in town loved to pick on anyone different, and Miles was certainly that. Therefore, he became the target of many a prank and sometimes even had rocks thrown at him. But he tried to ignore them and became even more inward and distant, avoiding people whenever possible.

CHAPTER 23

Concluding his business at the General Store, Franklin turned and bumped into Kathleen, who had been standing directly behind him waiting in line.

"Oh, excuse me, ma'am." He bent down to pick up his packages. He looked up and saw it was her. Gathering his wits about him, he managed to find his voice.

"Well, nice bumping into you again, ma'am." He smiled most pleasantly. He tried not to smile too much. He didn't want to seem forward or too eager. He studied her face and saw beauty the likes of which he hadn't seen since Pearly. She tugged at his heart.

Kathleen politely smiled at him.

"Is it? Mr...."

"Just call me Franklin, ma'am," he said, tipping his hat to her.

"All right, Frank," she said with a flair that made him grin.

"Franklin."

"Yes, well, don't you ever watch where you're going?"

"Apparently not when you're around, milady," he offered in amusement.

She didn't want to respond to that, but the corners of her mouth began to curl anyway. His eyes drew her in. They shined and twinkled. They always said that the eyes were the windows to the soul, and if that were true, she wanted to know more about him. He seemed charming enough. But unrefined. No matter, that can be fixed with time. He intrigued her.

"Perhaps you should try glasses, Frank."

"Franklin."

"Whatever. Thank you for not bruising me this time, and please try to be more careful in the future," she said, amused.

"I will do that, Miss…"

"Kathleen," she replied.

"Nice to meet you, Kathy."

"Kathleen."

"Whatever. It appears we are at a bit of an impasse here," he chuckled.

"It appears so."

"So, what do we do about it, Kathy?"

"I don't know about you, but to me, you do not look like a Franklin, sir. Your mother should have named you Frank, so therefore, you shall be called Frank by me!" she added so properly.

"Shall, huh?" His brow raised as he snickered. "All right, if that's the way you want it, Kathy, that's the way it shall be." He couldn't help himself. His snicker grew into a full-blown laugh.

She tried to look ruffled, but all she could do was laugh. She loved his laugh that seemed to come all the way from his gut. Low and loud, but not obnoxious. She liked that. A man who could laugh and see humor in the small things was rare in this day and age. It was charming and endearing. She studied his face and found wrinkles and lines that she was sure he had earned from years of labor. She had noticed his leg but didn't really bother her much. After all, he seemed strong and alive. She could see the muscles in his arms and his trim waist. But she did wonder how he had injured his leg and thought maybe one day he would tell her. Hoped he would tell her. Why was she feeling this way about him? She'd never been drawn to anyone like this before. She didn't understand and yet didn't have any more reservations about it.

Franklin wondered what she was thinking. He thought she was searching for something in his eyes. What did that mean? Did she have any interest in him at all, because he was certainly interested in her? Age had not dimmed her beauty—in fact, it seemed to heighten it. She had depth. He suspected there was a lot more to this woman than her fancy exterior, and he wanted to explore it.

"Well, Kathy," he said, "I must move on if I'm to get home anytime soon." He wanted to ask her to lunch or coffee or something that would be appropriate, but he figured it was too soon for that.

"I, too, have a full schedule," she replied. "Maybe we'll bump into each other again sometime."

"I would like that very much," he said as he smiled and tipped his hat to her.

"Well then, until next time, Frank." Her eyes sparkled, and she smiled as she proceeded down the boardwalk.

"Until next time, Kathy."

He limped off in the opposite direction, chuckling to himself. *Wow, this woman is something*, he mused.

Kathleen's heart thumped when she was near him and was disappointed that he didn't ask her to lunch. She really wanted to get to know this man who had taken her by surprise. So unlike anyone she had ever known and completely opposite her in almost every way. It puzzled her, but she dismissed it. She hoped their next meeting would be soon.

CHAPTER 24

As she poured herself a second cup of coffee, Maddie's thoughts turned toward what happened last night. How proud she was of Raff and how God had drawn him. She couldn't be happier, and her heart was full of thanksgiving and love for God and Raff.

A knock on the door brought her out of her reverie. She sat her coffee down and made her way to the door. Opening the door, she saw Raff smiling at her. Her heart caught in her throat. Wow! How could he possibly look even more handsome? She saw something on his face she'd never seen before. He was almost glowing, and his eyes were dancing. Her heart beat so loudly she was afraid Raff could hear it. *How can I not tell him?* Her heart ached for him to love her the way she loved him.

He stared at her, chuckling.

"Well, aren't you going to let me in," he asked in amusement.

Blushing, she giggled.

"Yes, of course. Come in."

She was so cute when she giggled like that. So feminine and beautiful. Stunning, really. Even with her hair a little askew and wearing an old dress, she still stole his heart. *I could love looking at her for a lifetime*, he thought.

"A…a little birdie told me you didn't have a Christmas tree yet," he declared.

"Wow! How very observant of you," she said, amused.

He laughed. "Come on, get your hat and coat and let's go find you a tree."

"Now?"

"No. Next week. Of course, now," he said with excitement. "The axe is in the car, and I know a place behind the farm where there are some beautiful specimens for lovely Christmas trees. Now, let's go!" he commanded.

His enthusiasm was infectious, and she grabbed her coat and hat, put on her boots, and they bounded out the door and down the stairs. He opened the car door for her.

Such a gentleman, she thought. "Since when have you ever been interested in Christmas?" she asked.

"Since last night, that's when." He was so happy to be with her and to simply enjoy life. Such a foreign feeling, this new joy. But oh so wonderful. He hoped it lasted a lifetime.

"Maddie, I can't tell you how much God has changed me in such a short amount of time. I feel like Christmas is the gift I've never received. One that is so amazing I can't wait to celebrate it."

"So, let's don't." She turned to him. "Raff, let's celebrate this season with everything in us. Let's get out the decorations, trim the tree, turn Christmas carols on the radio, and just be joyful and thankful. The love of God is a very powerful thing, and I can feel that that's what you are experiencing. It's amazing, and I want to cultivate that in you, not stifle it. Are you with me?"

"You bet I am! Let's go get us a tree before Christmas is over!"

"Christmas never has to be over, Raff. That's the beautiful thing about it. God is the gift that keeps on giving. That's why he sent his Son to die for us. He is the gift of Christmas!"

Raff shook his head. "Boy, do I have a lot to learn. I know so little, but I sure want to learn."

"That's what counts. You can't expect to learn it all right away. The Bible is a book that even if you've read it through a hundred times, there's always something to learn. And, if you're willing to, you will."

"Sounds a bit daunting."

"No, exciting!" She declared with a twinkle in her eye.

With the tree firmly in place and the boxes of decorations on the floor and furniture, they began with a string of colored lights. The tree was a six-foot noble fir. Its branches even and beautiful. It was a tree known for its lasting qualities as the needles stayed on for several weeks.

The radio was ringing with Christmas music and carols. Raff had heard most of them before but never had listened to the words or really understood what they'd meant until now. Christmas was something he began to treasure and wanted to remember every single moment of it.

With the lights in place, the ornaments were added. Most of them were handmade ones that Maddie had made as a child, but newer store-bought ones were added as well. Raff thought he liked the homemade ones the best. It showed Maddie's personality, what she was thinking and how she'd progressed during those years. He lapped it up like a dog with water. He couldn't get enough. He felt as though his heart couldn't contain much more, or it would burst with the joy of it all.

When the ornaments were completed, Maddie suggested they pop some corn and string it for a garland to place on the tree. He'd never heard or seen anything like that before but was game for anything.

As soon as the garland was on, it was time to plug in the lights! "Okay, Maddie, plug 'em in. Let's see those lights!"

The lights seemed to spread through the room with color and brilliance. The whole house seemed to ring with cheer. Raff clapped with delight. He was like a small child experiencing Christmas for the first time.

Maddie was delighting in his newly found joy and excitement. She was transfixed as she watched his eyes light up and dance.

"Raff, you're like a little kid. I love it!"

"I feel like a little kid… I guess. I've never had Christmas before, at least not that I remember. Dad wasn't into it at all. Mom tried in her own way to put up some greens, but no tree or color. It was pretty bland." His sadness was evident in his eyes.

"But this—this is incredible!" Excitement returned to his face and eyes.

"Hey, Maddie, let me take you to that little café in town to celebrate my first Christmas."

"Really?" She hoped he meant like a date, but probably more like a friend taking a friend. But she could live with that, for now. She wanted to share in the feelings he was having for the first time.

Raff wished he could tell her it was a date but wasn't sure that was proper. He didn't know how much longer he could go without telling her how he felt about her. He didn't want to scare her off, but he thought he had seen her eyes show interest in him more than once, but it might have just been wishful thinking.

"Of course. What a better way to celebrate?"

"Okay, I'd like that very much," she disclosed. She hoped that wasn't too forward. She wished she could tell him how she felt, but she was afraid. What if he still thought of her as a kid? That would hurt way too much.

They both bundled up and walked quickly to the car, both filled with anticipation and happiness.

The dinner at the café was lovely, and Raff enjoyed all the Christmas decorations that were around the room. The conversation was so easy and felt natural and fun. He wanted to take her in his arms but knew better.

The drive home was warm, and the radio was playing Christmas carols. It was simply delightful! After Raff parked the car, he opened her door and walked her to the door.

"Would you like to come in for a cup of coffee?" she asked.

Did he want to? Of course he wanted to. But he was afraid to. The way he was feeling right now, all he wanted to do was hold her and maybe kiss her the way he'd been dreaming about. He couldn't; rather, he wouldn't.

"I'd love to, but I have to get home. Thank you for everything, Maddie. I had a wonderful time today. You made it real special for me," he exclaimed. "I'll see you soon. Thanks again." He turned to leave.

He waved goodbye. He thought he saw just a second of disappointment in her eyes. Maybe there could be something between them if he were reading things right. His mind circled back to last night when she had hugged him. He wanted it to last forever. He loved the way their bodies fit together almost like they were made for each other.

It wasn't at all like the other women. This was real. He genuinely loved this girl with all his heart. He wanted to preserve her innocence, and he had begun to feel differently about how he wanted to use his own body too. Not just for his own selfish pleasure, but truly love a woman in a way he'd never known before. He had no idea that this was God's plan for him all along.

CHAPTER 25

May 1950

It had been two weeks since he had been to the river and wondered if his rod and reel were still on the bank where he left them. He'd love to have them back and maybe plan another fishing trip. Maybe actually get to fish this time. He was glad Kathleen was doing so well. He was grateful that he had been there to help.

Breakfast was underway. Eggs in the frying pan, along with three silver dollar pancakes and coffee was on the stove. Blueberry jam was on the table with butter, maple syrup, a plate, and silverware. He poured himself a cup of coffee just how he liked it—strong and black.

A knock came from the front door. He quickly flipped his eggs and pancakes and headed for the door. Opening it, he found a woman standing there who looked familiar but couldn't quite place her. Meticulously dressed right down to her high-heeled boots.

"Mr. Mayfield, I presume."

"You presumed correctly, ma'am. And who might you be?" For the life of him, he couldn't figure out why a woman of her obvious wealth would be standing at his front door.

She cleared her throat. "Mr. Mayfield, I am Kathleen Brennan. You might not recognize me this way because the last time you saw me, you were fishing me out of the river and pulling me up on the bank."

"Oh." The light dawned. "You're Miss Kathleen. How are you feeling now? You look rested and healthy. Are you? Did You suffer any lasting effects from the fall?"

"I am indeed well, thanks to you. I cannot thank you enough for being brave enough to come out that far in the rapids to rescue me. That took courage. You were willing to forfeit your own life for mine. That I will never forget."

"I assure you, ma'am, if I had time to think about the risks, you would not be here today. I just did what was necessary before the rapids took you."

"'Greater love hath no man than this; that a man lay down his life for a friend.' That's what you did for me. The very definition of a hero. There aren't that many around anymore. You, sir, are one of a kind."

He remembered his breakfast. "Please come in." He gestured for her to sit while he moved quickly toward the kitchen and walked to the stove. "I left my breakfast on the stove and need to turn it off before it's—too late!" He threw the pan in the sink. "Oh well, I wasn't that hungry anyway," he said painfully as he walked back into the living room.

"Oh, I'm so sorry I interrupted your breakfast. Let me take you to out to make up for it, please. I feel awful about it."

"No need. I'm fine. Would you like a cup of coffee? I didn't burn that...yet," he said, amused.

"I would like that very much, but I'm afraid I can't today. Rain check?"

"Of course. That would be nice," he said appreciatively.

"Mr. Mayfield..."

"George, ma'am. Just George."

"All right, George."

"You did a wondrous thing for me, and I would like to give you a little gift in my appreciation. It was my father's but isn't really something in which I'm interested. I thought that maybe it would enrich your life in a number of ways, and maybe you would treasure it as he did."

"No, ma'am. I do not need a reward for dragging you out of the water. Anyone close enough to hear you would have done it."

"You don't know that, and neither do I. Therefore, we will stick to the facts at hand. You did it. You gave me a second chance at life, and it is my pleasure and honor, sir, to give you this gift. It is a gift, and I will not take no for an answer! If you do not like it, I will find something else that might suit you better. Understood?"

"Yes, ma'am, but—"

"No buts, and please call me Kathleen."

"Kathleen, then. But I—"

"No buts. I want to do this for you. Please allow me to," she pleaded.

She opened the door and gestured for two men to come in. They were carrying a large chest that had been decorated beautifully. A treasure to be sure. But how could he accept something so beautiful? The men placed it on the floor, and Kathleen asked them to open it. Inside were dozens of books. First edition classics.

George gaped at the sight. "Kathleen, I cannot in all good conscience take this as payment. It is too marvelous and beautiful. Too much for me," he uttered.

"George Mayfield, now you listen to me," she said with the authority of a general. "This is a gift, not payment! Unless you hate books, my father would have been proud that such a man saved his daughter's life and would want you to have them. Do I make myself clear, sir? Besides," she softened, "you wouldn't want to hurt my feelings, would you?" she asked with a pout.

"In that case, Kathleen, I would be proud to do so and will care for them as your father obviously did. To be honest, I haven't been much of a reader, but I promise that I will be now! These are wonderful. How can I ever thank you?"

"It is I who is thanking you, sir. This is my pleasure, and I sincerely hope you enjoy them as my father did."

"Kathleen, I promise you I will do just that!"

"Then it is time for me to take my leave. Thank you again. I have thanked God for you ever since that day because I know he sent you there, and you answered his call."

"Pardon me, Kathleen, but I think it was your call I answered," he said with a smile.

Opening the door, she turned back to him and said, "Well said."

With that, she was gone, leaving George with a feeling he couldn't even identify. He started looking over the books, and with each one, his eyes filled with wonder. Now, he just needed a bookcase that would be worthy of those priceless books.

CHAPTER 26

December 1950

*T**hankfully*, Miles thought, *he was mostly working in the back room mixing compounds today. There were so many to mix and prescriptions to fill, and mercifully, there was a girl who was out front for shoppers.*

Days had passed since Raff had told him of the accident and borrowed his crowbar. He wondered if anyone was hurt and when, if ever, he would see his crowbar again.

He knew Raff wasn't a bad kid, just troubled with a father who didn't seem to care about him at all. Miles had felt a little sorry for him knowing some of his background. His pranks and teasing were just a way of letting off steam. He didn't like it, but certainly understood why.

He glanced at the calendar and realized that Christmas was just around the corner. Memories took him back to his childhood when Christmas was celebrated with excitement and beauty. He remembered his father chopping down a tree and the family decorating it with ornaments made from paper and other household items. There were a few ceramic and glass ones with shiny and beautiful reds, blues, greens, and golds. They'd strung the colored lights on the tree and placed boughs on the mantle and decorated with holly, ribbon, and candles. The room glowed with a variety of color and sparkle. They'd sung Christmas carols together, and the laughter from the house could be heard from outside. It was cheery and loving, and everyone had a wonderful time.

Christmas Eve, they'd open their stockings, which were usually filled with things like nuts, oranges, peppermint sticks, and something with which to play. So lovely, and his father and mother would watch with delight at the scene. A bit chaotic, but that was part of the Christmas spirit his parents treasured and fostered in their children.

His parents had been gone for years, and all the traditions and joy had gone with them. He just didn't possess the spirit needed to get into Christmas or the desire to spend time decorating. He'd never collected any ornaments or bought any lights. Christmas was just fine for others. For him, it was just another day, except he did get the day off. He didn't necessarily hate Christmas; it just didn't have anything to do with him. He wasn't religious at all but had nothing against it—just hadn't ever gone to church before, and wasn't inclined to go now.

He just had one more prescription to fill, then he could finally go home. It seemed the day had crawled by, and he was tired. He longed to sit in his chair by the fire and relax. He had some leftovers he could throw in the oven, eat, and go to bed. He needed a good night's sleep. Tomorrow was his day off. He wanted to clean up the barn a little and organize his tools, which had needed to be done for months. Now he was ready to take on that project—if it wasn't too cold outside.

CHAPTER 27

Wondering what Raff might be doing, Maddie grabbed her Bible by the stand. She started to open it, but her thoughts scattered. She wondered when she would see him again. She knew they were supposed to spend time together so she could answer questions about God, but was hoping it would have been before now. It had been days since she'd heard anything from him. She knew he needed to spend time going through his father's papers, but how long could that take?

She couldn't read. Couldn't concentrate. And the Bible deserved her full attention. She glanced at the clock and noticed it was almost dinnertime. It became dark so early this time of year, which only made the evenings longer and lonelier. However, that's also when she enjoyed her own Christmas decorations the most. The lights always seemed to cheer her.

Her stomach growled, and she hated the thought of cooking for herself. Sometimes cooking for one just seemed like too much trouble. She looked in the fridge for leftovers. She had made some meat loaf the night before; she could fix herself a meat loaf sandwich. She pulled out the meat, mayo, mustard, butter and retrieved the bread from the bread box on the counter. That's when she heard the knock. She sighed.

She walked to the door believing it was another salesman. The encyclopedia guy had just come through the day before and a vacuum cleaner person the day before that. She couldn't think what might be next. Maybe some guy selling vitamins or brushes.

Opening the door, she was startled to see Raff standing there with a big grin on his face. Her heart started beating wildly. *Calm down*, she told herself.

"Raff, it's so good to see you. I was just thinking about you."

"You were," he answered, thinking maybe things were looking up. *She was thinking about me! That sounds like progress.* It cheered his heart.

"Come on in."

He was already halfway through the door. Unintentionally, he brushed her arm as he passed. It sent a tingle through him. He wanted to grab her and pull her to him, but instead, he found his chair and sat down.

Maddie shivered with the touch. A good kind of shiver and wanted more.

"Have you had dinner yet?" she asked. "I was just going to make myself a meat loaf sandwich, and I think I have enough for two if you're interested."

"That sounds great. I'm starving. Besides, I have something I'd like to talk through with you. Maybe you can help me figure out something that just doesn't make sense to me. Two heads are better than one, they say," he said cheerfully.

"They do, huh? Who's they?"

"Don't know, but there is some truth to it, don't you think?"

She shrugged. "I suppose. I'd love to help you, if I can."

"Good."

"Come on, let's get a bite to eat." They walked into the kitchen, and Maddie took plates and silverware out and pulled out two more slices of bread.

"So tell me what's on your mind," she said as she started making the sandwiches.

He wanted everything but the mustard.

"It's about my dad."

"Go on."

"The desk is stacked with overdue bills that go back at least three years. It's thousands of dollars. Here's the kicker. Dad has a floor-to-ceiling bookcase full of first edition books—the classics in mint condition."

Maddie's brows furrowed. "Wow, I didn't know your parents had any money."

"Me either. He could have paid off those debts with just a few of those books. They're priceless. So why didn't he?"

"That doesn't make any sense at all," she said.

"And there's more," he said, continuing. "When I was looking through the desk, a drawer got stuck. I found an envelope underneath it containing a skeleton key with no note or any word about what it might open."

"That's so weird," she said as she continued with the sandwiches. "There doesn't seem to be any rhyme or reason to any of it."

Raff sighed. "I know. It has me stumped. I do know the only way I can pay off the debt is by selling the farm," he said, shaking his head.

"So, that means you'd be moving away again," she said with disappointment.

"You know, Maddie. When I first came home, that's what I was planning to do, but I'm changing my mind. I think maybe if I could find a way to keep the farm and stay here, I will."

"Really, Raff?" Her heart nearly leapt out of her chest. Her knees became weak, so she quickly sat down before she fell.

"Really. And if I can be honest with you, I like living next door to you. I love our talks, and I feel...well, I feel closer to you than I ever have," he said. He placed his hand over hers. He circled her hand with his own.

Tell her, his heart was screaming. *Tell her you love her.*

They stared at each other. Their eyes intent on trying to see what the other was feeling.

Maddie closed her eyes as that shiver that started at her feet climbed all the way to her heart, which was beating wildly. She was sure he could hear it.

Oh no, he thought. *I said too much.* He withdrew his hand and placed it in his lap.

"Maddie, I'm sorry. I shouldn't have done that." The ache in his heart only strengthened every time he saw her. How was he going to keep seeing her when he wanted to be with her. Wanted to tell her that he loved her with all his heart. Disappointment cut him to his very soul. He grieved that she didn't feel the same way.

"Raff. No, please don't apologize. It's okay." She could see that he was hurt, but she didn't know why. Why did he pull away just when she thought they were getting somewhere? She stood and plated the sandwiches, filled the water glasses, and handed them to him. Then placed her plate in front of her.

She bowed her head and asked the Lord to bless the food and thanked him for their many blessings. When she was finished, she searched Raff's face and tried to see any indication of his feelings. At least he said he wanted to be next door to her. That seemed like an improvement. She wanted to tell him how much she loved him.

But he didn't seem to feel the same way.

They focused on the mystery in front of them.

"Raff, would it be okay if I were to come over to your house to take a look at the stuff in the office? Maybe we can figure it out together." Hope filled her eyes.

"Yes, of course. That would be great." He smiled at her. "How about tomorrow morning? I'll take you to breakfast, since you just fixed my dinner, then come home and start working. How does that sound?" He asked cheerfully. Desperately hoping she would say yes.

"I'd love to. Pick me up at around…say nine-thirty or so."

He agreed.

The rest of the dinner went well, and they seemed to enjoy each other. Again, the conversation came easily, and the time flew by. Raff helped her with the dishes. She washed. He dried. Laughter rang through the kitchen and raised both their spirits. By the time Raff looked at his watch, it was ten-thirty.

"Oh my goodness. Time went by so fast I didn't realize how late it is. I need to go."

All the way to the door, Raff thought about what he wanted to say to her. *Should I risk it?* he wondered. What if she didn't want that kind of relationship? At least then he would know for sure. If she didn't, they could still be friends—good friends. *We get along so well, and she seems to like being with me*, he argued.

When they got to the door, he grabbed her and pulled her into his arms. She didn't resist. She came willingly. She looked up into his face. He tucked her hair behind her ear. Tracing her chin and neck and then her lips with his fingers, he could feel her warm breath on his face. Slowly, he bent down and brushed his lips against hers. It took her breath away. Having waited so long for this, he kissed her again, with abandon. Not only was he not disappointed, but it was amazing!

She fell into his arms and leaned against him. His kiss felt like heaven. She didn't want it to end.

Raff pushed away.

"Maddie, I have something I need to tell you. I... I'm... Well, I'm in love with you."

He studied her. "I'm sorry if that's not how you feel, but I thought you should know. I think I've been in love with you since the accident. But, if you just want to be friends, I understand."

She pulled him back down and kissed him. "Does that tell you anything? Raff Mayfield? I've been in love with you since I was seven years old."

They looked at each other and laughed with relief.

"Okay," he said. "Now what do we do?"

"We work together and get your farm out of debt and take it one day at a time, that's what we do."

He hugged her again.

"And with that, my sweet, I have got to go. Any more kissing tonight, and I'd be in trouble." He kissed her on the forehead. "I'll see you tomorrow," he said and walked out the door.

On the front porch, Maddie raised her voice. "Tomorrow." She waved to him, and he responded with a wave and a good night.

CHAPTER 28

Trying to find a reason to go into town, Franklin looked in the fridge. He was out of butter, and there was no bread in the bread box. *Can't have sandwiches without bread and butter*, he thought.

Now how to "bump" into Kathleen. His thoughts seem to be about her so often lately. He couldn't concentrate on anything but Kathy, so he gave up and decided to go into town.

He wished he had set a time to meet her somewhere. It would've been so much easier. *What if she isn't even in town?* he thought. *What if I can't find her at all? I don't know where she lives or how to find her. There's got to be a way.*

Franklin looked for her in the General Store where he bought a few items—more than what was on his original list. That seemed to happen more often than not. He checked the boardwalk, the café, and the dress shop. Nothing.

To say that Franklin was disappointed would be an understatement. He missed her, which seemed impossible since he really didn't know her. But there was something about her that made him feel like he'd known her his whole life.

He walked to his '39 Ford pickup and turned to get into the car. He looked toward the boardwalk up and down the street one more time, then gave up. He sighed and opened the door, hitting Kathleen and landing her on her backside.

"Really, Frank, why do you insist on putting me in the hospital?" she asked, looking very upset.

"Kathy, I'm so sorry." He helped her get to her feet. "I didn't see you there."

"Well, Frank, it's nice to know you weren't aiming for me, although I have to admit I'm starting to feel like a target," she said sternly, until she giggled. "I'm fine, but I expect you to take me dinner to apologize and help heal my bruised ego and...other parts," she said, laughing.

"I can't think of anything I would enjoy more," he said cheerfully.

She took his arm and strode down the walk toward the new Italian restaurant in town. He couldn't believe his luck. He was certain he had missed her. He watched as she gingerly sat down on the chair. He saw her wince when he seated her, then he scooted her under the table.

"Kathy, are you sure you're all right?" he asked. "I'm so very sorry I hit you. Do you need to see a doctor?"

"Frank, stop fussing. It's just that my tuchus is a little sore," she said with a tinge of embarrassment.

He raised an eyebrow. "Tuchus?" he asked, laughing.

There is that adorable laugh again. He is someone I really want to know better, she reasoned. He was easy to talk with—nothing awkward or forced. She loved that and felt totally relaxed.

He was having such a good time. It had been a long time since he felt like this. He thought he might feel guilty about being with another woman, but Pearly had been gone a long time, and all those old thoughts vanished with Kathleen's laughter. Too soon it was time to part company.

"Kathy, um...do...do you think I could call on you sometime? Maybe pick you up and go out to eat or something? I know my pickup isn't exactly what you're used to, but I promise it will be clean and shine like the sun before I let your little tuchus sit on my seat." There was just a hint of a blush as he stammered through his invitation.

"Is that what they call a date, Frank?" she asked, amused.

"That depends."

"On what?"

"Do you want it to be?" he asked shyly with a broad smile.

"Maybe," she replied coyly.

"So, is that a yes or a no, Miss Kathleen?"

"That, Frank, is a definite yes," she said with a smile on her lips and in her eyes.

He went home with his head in the clouds and a chuckle in his heart. He couldn't wait for their first date. Now, he just had to figure out what that would be. Something unexpected and a little romantic. He had no ideas at all.

CHAPTER 29

Raff was right on time. He was always punctual. He couldn't wait to see Maddie. He was excited that they were finally on the same page. She loved him. She really loved him. His heart sang with joy. Maybe they could even begin to plan a life together. Too soon. It was enough right now to know she had longed for him in the same way he had for her.

He drove up her driveway and parked. Opening the car door, he got out, closed the door, and walked up the steps to the front porch. He was about to knock on the door when it opened.

"Raff, I'm glad to see you." She wrapped her arms around him and hugged him.

"Well, good morning to you, my sweet," he said, chuckling. "It's good to see you."

Maddie pushed back and said, "Okay, enough with the pleasantries. Come on, I'm starving!"

Raff laughed. "I get it. Some things are far more important than romance."

"That's right," she said with a giggle. "Let's go."

"You always were a good eater and rarely full. All right, let's get going."

They drove to the café, both so pleased in their newly reciprocated love. It seemed so much easier and natural without all that angst that had existed. It was finally out in the open and felt right and good.

The café was still in the middle of the morning rush but had a couple empty booths open. The waitress told them to seat themselves and that she'd be right with them.

They looked into each other's eyes and saw a happiness that was apparent to anyone that looked at them. She fairly glowed with love.

"So, Maddie Henderson, how are you feeling today?" he asked with a knowing smile on his face.

She smiled shyly. "I feel like my life has radically changed, which makes me very happy. I can't believe we both felt the same way but didn't feel like the other was ready for it," she said, shaking her head.

"I know, but it all worked out, and I'm crazy about you, darlin'," he declared. "I've never been happier."

He held her hands across the table.

Interrupting them, the waitress gave them their menus. "Coffee?"

"Yes, please," they said together.

"How would you like it?"

"Black," they said in unison.

The waitress filled both cups, giving them time to study the menus. "I'll give you a few minutes to decide and be right back," she said as she walked to her next station.

As they were reading, Raff reached his hand over to Maddie and wove his fingers through hers. They both looked up and smiled as their eyes met, which told the whole story.

When the waitress returned, they gave their orders, sat back, and just reveled in each other.

When the food came, Maddie was more than ready to dive in, but Raff stopped her and said he'd like to pray over breakfast.

Maddie was so pleased and told him that she would love that.

"Jesus," Raff began, "I want to thank you for all you've done for me. Thank you for this food, and especially thank you for Maddie. Amen."

Blushing, Maddie began eating her plate of sausage patties, scrambled eggs, and toast. Raff's plate held two eggs over easy, hash browns, and toast.

It wasn't long before breakfast was over, and they headed back to Raff's farm. They were anxious to find anything that would give them a clue into his father's affairs.

As Maddie walked through the door of the farm, her eyes glanced around the room. Even though it sort of looked the same, it was more run-down and in disrepair. She felt sorry for Raff knowing what that meant for him—the work involved. When it came time for him to tackle that part of this home, she would be right by his side.

Raff moved the desk chair and brought another one into the office for Maddie. She looked at the desk and then at the books behind it. She read the titles with awe and appreciation. "Wow, what I wouldn't give to have all these books," she murmured. "You're right about these being priceless classics."

"Maddie, you can borrow as many as you want to read, but if I can save the farm without having to sell them, that would be my first goal," he pledged.

"Oh, I agree. This is a collection that you want to hold on to and even pass down to the next generation. This is something that is rare and wonderful. No, we will find a way to keep them—all of them," she swore.

They began by reading each invoice on the desk. There were several of the businesses he didn't recognize, though he didn't know all of them from neighboring towns.

"Maddie. Look at this one. Do you recognize it?"

"I don't think so, but I don't know all the farming communities and the businesses."

"Hmm. Yeah, that makes sense, I guess," he said. "Maybe I'm just grasping at straws."

"No, you have to search like that, with questions. Everything is new, and we're just trying to make sense of it. Don't try to sec-ond-guess yourself. Go with your gut." A few seconds passed. "Wait! We need to stop right now and pray. We can't do this in our own wisdom. We need God to give us his. He says in his Word that if we ask for wisdom, he will give it to us. We really need that right now." They bowed their heads, and Raff began to pray.

"Dear God, we need you right now. We don't fully understand what we're looking for. Please give us your eyes and wisdom so we can find a way to save this farm, my home. Thank you for all you've done for us and showing us how much we love each other. We know beyond any doubt that it is a gift from you. Amen."

"That was beautiful, Raff. Thank you," she said with sparkling eyes. "I'm so proud of you and the way you are changing. I've wanted this for so long, and I'm so happy that God chose to draw you to himself, and you responded. I can't wait to see how you grow spiritually."

"Thanks. Frankly, I'm in awe of this whole process and wonder what comes next," he responded.

They looked into each other's eyes, and then Raff quickly looked away. He took a deep breath. "Well, if we're going to get anything done today, we'd better get back to work." If he looked any longer at her up close and personal like, he would want to kiss her. They needed to keep their minds on the project at hand, and he was glad for the distraction.

They continued looking through the papers, inspecting each one for anything unusual. After a couple hours, Raff suggested they take a break and have a cup of coffee.

He put some on the stove and stepped into the living room, where Maddie was already seated on the couch by the front window. Both lost in thought, Raff smelled the coffee and walked to the kitchen, poured two cups, and brought them out to the living room, placing one on the end table near Maddie and one on his side table next to the chair.

"Raff, when you got home, you said your lawyer told you that you needed to come home and settle the estate. Maybe we should go and talk with him. Maybe he knows something we don't," she offered.

"That's a great idea! I'll call and make an appointment. Who knows? We might even be able to get in today, although I doubt it," he added.

"Never know, it's worth a shot. At least make an appointment for as early as we can get in," she said.

Raff rose from his chair and walked back into the office, grabbed the phone, and dialed the operator.

"Number please," a woman answered with a nasal quality to her voice.

"I'm trying to find a number for a lawyer named Lucas Sprat, can you help me with that?"

"Of course, sir. Hold on while I look it up." A few seconds went by, when she asked if he had a pencil.

"Yes, ma'am, I do. Go ahead."

"The number is 555-1258. Have a good day, sir." Raff wrote them down as she reeled off the numbers.

"Thank you, ma'am. It just might be looking better already. Thanks." He hung up.

"Okay, we have our first step. I'll go call right now."

When he returned, he had a smile on his face. "This afternoon at four. Let's hope we get somewhere."

"I hope so, too."

CHAPTER 30

Lucas was seated at his desk doing paperwork when Loretta knocked on the door.

"What do you want, Loretta? I'm busy!" he growled.

She opened it to tell him that he had an appointment at four with Raff Mayfield.

"Good. It's about time. I need him to sign some papers. Get his farm settled," he said thoughtfully.

"Yes, Mr. Sprat."

"Just tell me when he arrives. Oh, and bring in some coffee," he said gruffly.

"Yes, sir." She turned to leave and walked through the door back to her desk.

The clock on the wall said three-thirty, so he needed a little time to prepare. He put his other papers and yelled.

"Loretta, bring me the Mayfield file!" he screeched.

"Be right in, sir."

"Well, hurry up, I don't have all day!"

"Yes, sir," she groaned. Why did he have to get so nasty? She was doing the best she could.

His chair squeaked as he moved around. His figure showed years of neglect and more than a few meals out, probably most with alcohol. He had lived the "good life," and it showed on his face and body. His wrinkles were pronounced for fifty-three, and his hair circled the back of his head with a spot in front that shined liked the sun. He'd fancied himself a ladies' man, but most women only hung around him for his money. He walked with a cane; he thought it made him look austere.

He was grouchy, ill-tempered, and most of all wealthy. His business had done very well and had clients from all over the area. Being a business attorney had served him well, and he had property, a classic car collection, and a mansion with servants to care for his every whim.

"Mr. Sprat, Mr. Mayfield is here to see you, sir."

"Thank you, Loretta, please send him in, and would you please bring some coffee with cream and sugar. I would appreciate it," he said sweetly.

"Of course, sir. Be right back." She left the room and ushered in Raff and Maddie.

Lucas looked up. "Raff, I see you brought someone with you. How nice," he said.

"Yes, this is Maddie, she's helping me with the farm and tying up loose ends," he informed him.

"Very good. Very good," he said quickly.

His eyes didn't look like he thought it was very good at all, thought Maddie.

"Now, Raff, all you have to do is sign right here, and everything will be taken care of."

Raff's brows furrowed. "Mr. Sprat…"

"Call me Lucas, all my friends do. We don't have to be so formal, now do we? I was pretty close to your father, so I feel as though I already know you."

Maddie thought he sounded insincere.

"Okay, Lucas. The reason I'm here…"

"Here's the pen, and all you have to do is sign right here," he repeated, as he pointed to the signature line.

"Lucas, the reason I'm here is because I have some questions I'd like to ask you," he said a little impatiently.

Loretta opened the door. "I have your coffee, sir." She brought in a tray containing two cups of coffee, cream, and sugar and set it down on the desk.

"Thank you, Loretta."

"You're welcome, sir." She turned and left, shutting the door behind her.

"Please help yourself to the coffee," he said.

"No, thank you," they said together.

"Okay. Questions, you say," he asked nervously.

"Yes, something that I don't understand."

Maddie studied Lucas's face as Raff talked to him.

"Do you have any idea why my father never paid any of his bills? When I came home, there was two to three years of bills on his desk. How could that happen?"

"I'm sure I don't know. That just doesn't sound like him at all," he replied. "Just how much debt are we talking about here?"

"Thousands. Look, I want to keep the farm, and unless I can pay the debt, I may have to sell," he answered, sadness covering his face.

"Oh, what a shame. Such sad news. I'm so very sorry to hear that," he said, shaking his head with concern. "But I have no idea why your father didn't take care of those things."

Raff dropped his head. "So, what do I do now?"

"Well, I hate to say it, but you could be right. You'll have to sell the farm." He was shaking his head sadly. "As much as it pains me to say it."

Maddie abruptly stood up and put out her hand to shake his. "Thank you, Mr. Sprat. We'll be in touch." She turned to Raff. "We have to go," she said tersely.

"Maddie...?"

"Now, Raff!" She turned and walked out the door with Raff trying to catch up.

"Maddie, stop! I wasn't through! I don't understand! What is it? Will you stop, please?"

Lucas started after them, yelling, "Wait, Raff. You didn't sign those papers..."

Too late, they were out of reach. He turned and went to his office slinging a string of curse words Loretta hadn't heard before.

Maddie stopped and turned to Raff.

"Raff, there is something about that man that makes my skin crawl. He sounded nice enough, but did you see his eyes? He was nervous, and… I don't know, but I didn't believe what he was saying," she said emphatically.

"I don't know, he seemed okay to me," he replied.

"Didn't you see how many times he asked you to sign the papers?"

Raff's brow arched. "Well, yes, now that you mention it. Why?"

"He was just a little too eager. Like there was something personal at stake…something like that. It didn't seem right."

She was steaming, and when Raff took the time to rehearse the conversation, he could see her point. "I wonder what he wanted me to sign?"

"I don't know, but I think we're going to have to find our answers somewhere else."

"Where?"

"Don't know, but there's something shady about him. I can feel it in my bones."

"Maddie, I trust your judgment. You've always been able to read people, I've seen it," he said softly.

She laughed. "Yeah, except you. Totally missed that one." She smiled.

He chuckled. "Well, no one's a hundred percent right."

They walked to the car, Raff opened the doors, and they got in.

"What do you say we go get a BLT before we go home. I'm hungry."

"You're always hungry." She laughed. "But I could eat a sandwich and fries, maybe a strawberry shake, onion rings. Let's go!"

CHAPTER 31

F ranklin knocked on the door. Nervously, he stood and waited for
it to open. It was several seconds before Hettie opened it.

"Well, ya must be Frank. Kathleen will be down in jes' a minute," she said with her usual flair and smile. Her brow lifted, giving
him the once-over.

It seemed she felt like she was in on some secret to which he
wasn't a party.

"Franklin, ma'am," he said, nodding.

"C'mon in." She motioned for him to come inside.

"Thank you, very much," he said as he walked past her and
looked around. He couldn't believe what this place looked like. He'd
never seen a home that had so much luxury and finery. *Holy cow,* he
thought, *I knew she was wealthy, but this is amazing!*

Oak hardwoods throughout the house. On the walls in the hall
was Asian floral wallpaper in blues and lavenders. The calla lilies had
extremely long stems on a cream background with mint-green sword
ferns and a dark-green narrow stripe separating the rows. The Persian
rug down the hall was wide, but not all the way to the walls, and had
a beige background with pine-green and pale-blue flowers and ran
the length of the long hall.

He looked up as Kathleen walked lightly down the steps, her
posture erect, without being stiff. She looked like a model. She was
wearing an Audrey Hepburn dress that had a black velvet long-sleeved
bodice with a modest V-neck and a full skirt with a black background

and white circles, topped off with black heels with a bow, and she was absolutely beaming. "Wow!" he exclaimed. "You look stunning!"

He smiled at her and was so proud that she would want to be with him.

"Why, thank you, kind sir," she said shyly. "Frank, you shaved off your beard," she marveled.

"I did." He beamed. "Like it?" He felt his naked face, still feeling strange. And cold.

"I do. You look so handsome." She walked over and felt his face, tracing her fingers along his jawline. "First time I've seen you so finely dressed, too. It becomes you," she said coyly.

"Why, Miss Kathleen Brennan, are you flirting with me?"

"I believe I am, sir. Do you mind?" she coquettishly asked.

"Not even one little bit!" He chuckled.

He was wearing a white shirt with a black bolo tie, a blue jacket, and black trousers. He also had a black topcoat over the suit. She thought he had never looked so handsome. She was captivated.

"So where are we going?" she asked, as she handed him her coat and he slipped it on, adding a scarf and stocking cap.

"Wouldn't you like to know?"

"Yes, sir, I would." She smiled, looking up at him. Their eyes met, and they held the gaze. He took a deep breath and turned away.

"Shall we go, Kathy?" he asked with a smile on his face, offering his arm.

Taking his arm, she answered, "We shall, Frank."

Hettie opened the door for them, smiling that broad smile of hers.

"You kids have fun now, ya hear," she said, chuckling. "Oh, and be home by midnight, Kathleen." She laughed.

"Hettie!" she shouted.

Hettie roared with laughter as she closed the door. "Well, if that ain't somethin'! She's as smitten as the day is long. My, oh my," she said, lifting both hands to her face. "This is goin' to be fun to watch. My Kathleen's fin'lly in love! If that don't beat all. He ain't bad-lookin'," she said, shaking her head.

Franklin escorted her to the shining red pickup and opened the door. It was sparkling. Not a spot or speck of dirt anywhere. He patted the seat and turned to her.

"Just put that little tuchus of yours right here, Kathy." He chuckled.

She was laughing as she took Franklin's hand and climbed up into the truck.

"Very funny." Her eyes danced as she gazed at him.

She was drop-dead gorgeous, and he couldn't believe she was actually going with him on a date. Incredible! He could hardly take his eyes off her or concentrate on anything else. Her eyes were inviting and warm and beautiful.

"All right, Frank, tell me where we're going."

"Nope, you'll see."

"You Franklin Atwood, are full of surprises," she smiled expectantly.

He drove her to town and parked on the street where a man stood on the walk waiting. Franklin nodded at him, and he walked away.

"What are we doing here, Frank?"

"Kathleen Brennan, will you try to be patient, please?" he implored.

"I'm trying, Frank. I'm just excited." She felt as giddy as a schoolgirl. This was a feeling she'd never had before, and she liked it. A lot. Truthfully, she was crazy about this man. He was so handsome and charming and wonderful and exciting. And he'd even shaved for her. She knew that couldn't have been easy, and she never would have asked him to, but it made him even more attractive and irresistible. She hoped he felt the same way. Oh, how she hoped so.

A horse with a sleigh pulled up beside the pickup. Frank opened the door, walked around the front, and opened hers. He helped her down to the sidewalk.

Finally seeing the sleigh, her excitement heightened.

"Oh, Frank, this is wonderful," she exclaimed. "I can't believe you did this."

"Just one of my many charms," he said, smirking. He grabbed a bag that was under the seat.

"Come, Miss Kathleen, your carriage awaits."

"Kathy."

"Whatever."

They laughed as he helped her up into the sleigh. She scooted over, allowing room for Franklin. He got up and sat down next to her. He pulled out a blanket from under the seat and placed it on their laps, telling the driver to go ahead.

"Yes, sir," he said, nodding. They started moving.

Franklin opened the bag and pulled out a thermos and a large cup. He opened the thermos, handed the cup to Kathleen, and filled it with hot chocolate. Then poured some into the thermos lid.

"I hope you like hot chocolate," he said with a grin.

"I love it and rarely have it. Thank you. You've thought of everything."

"Not quite. If you can stand it, there's more."

It started snowing. *How convenient*, he thought. *Maybe cuddling will happen automatically. I couldn't have ordered it any better if I tried.* His lips curled up.

"Oh, it's beautiful." She started to shiver.

"Cold?" he asked. He looked at her, and she nodded. He reached over and pulled her closer to him. She rested her head on his shoulder.

She couldn't believe how romantic he was being, and she loved it. He made her heart soar. Being this close to him gave her goose bumps. She never wanted the ride to end.

He loved the way it felt having her so close to him. He looked into her face and eyes. Course, it was getting dark, so he really couldn't see her eyes. But he could see her mouth and suddenly wanted to kiss her. He thought it was too soon, but the pull was very strong. He kissed her on the cheek.

"Frank," she whispered.

"Yes, my dearest," he said sweetly.

"Can we stay like this forever?"

"Of course, if you don't mind freezing to death."

"As long as I'm with you, I wouldn't care," she said dreamily.

"We're almost there." He was smiling broadly. "Are you ready for part two?" he asked.

"You know how I love surprises, Frank," she said, smiling.

"So far, so good, then."

CHAPTER 32

B ack in the office again, Raff was restless. His thoughts turned to Maddie. His heart was so full of love for this woman. Not only did he love her, but he respected and admired her. He wanted nothing more than to spend a lifetime waking up beside her every morning, spending time building a life and family together.

But it was too soon to be thinking like that. They barely confessed their love for each other. He couldn't believe how hard and fast he'd fallen for her, but then, he'd known her forever—except the last five years. The years when she turned into the most beautiful, amazing woman. Sighing, he saw the skeleton key on the desk.

He picked it up and inspected it again. What did it open, and where would he find it? What else was his dad hiding, and what would be so important that it would need a key? More questions. The biggest question was how to pay off the debt. He could sell some of those books, and all this angst would be over, but he really felt he should keep the collection together. So maybe he could get a loan from the bank. But how? He had no collateral except the farm. Maybe he could sell just a piece of it. The part where the stream is. No, that wouldn't work either. He couldn't give up that part. He raked his hands through his hair and slammed his fist on the desk. *This is impossible*, he thought. His head pounded.

All these questions were driving him crazy. He couldn't put the pieces together; they were just unattached parts that made no sense at all. He tried to concentrate, but just couldn't. He was through thinking about this. His head was like a hammer that pounded with every single heartbeat. He headed to the bathroom for some aspirin in the medicine cabinet. He reached for it as he glanced toward his dad's prescriptions again. What was that one? He picked it up and read the label. "Axert. I wonder what that is and why he was taking it." He furrowed his brow and tilted his head. *Strange*, he thought. But then everything about his dad was strange, why should this be any different?

He started to put it back on the shelf when he had an idea. He grabbed all three of them. Placing them in his trousers pocket, he strode to the living room to get his coat and boots on. He headed out the door and down the steps over to the car. The day was filled with blue sky and sunshine, but bitterly cold. It was well below freezing, with a breeze that made the cold go right through him. He raised the collar on his coat, opened the car door, and sat down. Starting the car, he backed it out of the driveway and drove down the road toward town.

As he walked through the door, the bell hanging over the door rang. He walked up to the counter where the cashier was and asked if he could talk to the pharmacist.

"Sure," she said. "I'll go get him for you and be right back." She turned back out of sight, and Raff perused the store while he was waiting.

"He'll be right out, sir."

"Fine, thank you."

He continued looking around. There were Christmas decorations all throughout the store—actually, all through town and all the stores. He just hadn't noticed it before.

"May I help you, sir?" he asked.

Raff turned and walked up to the counter. His jaw dropped. He hadn't even realized he was staring.

"Um… Mr. Strattford, you're the pharmacist?" he asked, in complete shock. His thoughts raced as he tried to recover without totally embarrassing himself.

"I am. Do I know you?"

"I'm Raff," he confessed. He hoped he didn't sound like that boy who had pestered him for years.

"Raff, how good to see you," he said cheerfully.

"It is?" he asked in astonishment.

"Of course. How are you? I'm so sorry about your dad," he offered.

"Ah, yeah, thanks." He bowed his head. He needed to apologize for all those years of abuse he'd inflicted on this man, now that he was face-to-face with him. But he needed to do it before he lost his nerve.

"Mr. Strattford, sir, I need to apologize to you for all those years I was so nasty to you. I shouldn't have done that, and I knew it all along. Can you ever forgive me?" he asked, with remorse in his eyes.

"I appreciate the apology, son, but I understand. And yes, I will forgive you. I made a pretty good target if I were to be truthful."

"I'm so sorry. I can assure you that I'm not that kid anymore," he declared.

"I'm sure that's true. A boy has to grow up some time," he said with a warm smile. "No fretting, I hold no ill will toward you at all."

"That's very gracious of you considering what I've done. I thank you for your kindness, sir. I don't deserve it."

"Consider it over and forgotten," he said with such warmth that Raff thought he might even like this guy.

Miles offered his hand to Raff to shake in an unspoken bond of forgiveness, and Raff responded with abandon. *Forgiveness is a powerful thing*, he thought.

"So, how can I help you, Raff?"

"Oh." He pulled out all the prescriptions from his pocket and handed them to him.

"My dad was taking all these prescriptions. Can you tell me what they're for?"

Miles looked at all of them, then looked up at Raff.

"He was taking all these together?" he asked tentatively.

"I guess so. They were all on the same shelf together. Why? Is there something wrong?"

"These two are for a heart condition, but this one is for migraines."

"Migraines! I don't think Dad ever had migraines."

"These things should never be taken together!" he said emphatically.

"Why is that?"

"Because this can cause a faster heartbeat and constrict blood vessels, and if taken enough of them at one time, or over a period of time, could very well cause a heart attack!"

"Really. Then why would any doctor or pharmacist give them to him? That makes no sense."

"I don't know. No reputable pharmacist would fill that knowing what he was already taking. But if he took it to one who didn't know his history, he might."

"As far as I know, he always took it to the same place. He was very much a creature of habit," Raff said with a tinge of anger.

"Yes, I can believe that knowing your father just a little bit," he acknowledged.

"Raff, I hate to ask this, but did your father have any enemies?"

"I don't think so." His brow arched. "Are you thinking what I think you're thinking?" he asked incredulously.

"I'm saying that it might not hurt to take this to the police just to make sure."

His brow raised. "My father was not a nice guy, but I don't think anyone hated him enough to do something like this."

"Maybe not. I'm just saying it might help you figure this out more quickly. Save a few steps. That's all I'm saying," he said, thinking of the questions Raff had.

"Wow! That's a lot to think about," he said, shaking his head. "Thanks, Mr. Strattford." Raff turned to leave.

"Raff. Here's the prescriptions back."

"Thanks."

"I never did ask you if anyone was hurt in that accident the other night."

"Not really, just a bad goose egg on her head and a huge headache. I took her to emergency just to make sure. She just had to rest for a couple days," he said.

"About my crowbar…"

"Oh, yeah. I haven't forgotten. It's just that I dropped it in the snow in such a hurry to get her out of the car, and there's still so much snow in the ditch, I haven't looked for it yet. But I will as soon as the snow melts, I promise I'll get it back to you," he explained.

"I'm not too concerned about it, I just wanted to remind you. Oh, and I owe you a big apology."

"What on earth for?"

"The little shooting incident. I would never have hurt you, I just wanted to scare you a little," he said with a smile and raised brow.

"Well, that you did accomplish," he said, chuckling. "I know you well enough to know if you wanted me dead, I would have been. You're a crack shot, sir. I remembered that."

"You're right on both counts," he nodded with a smile.

"Thanks again, Mr. Strattford. I don't know yet what I'm going to do about this, but I thank you for the information." And with that, Raff turned and walked to the door. He turned and waved goodbye.

"Goodbye, Raff, and good luck. If you ever need help with anything, I'm not that far away."

"Thanks for the offer, I appreciate it. Who knows, I might take you up on it. And thanks for the information, too." He walked out the door.

CHAPTER 33

The sleigh pulled up to the barn. It was decorated with lights everywhere. There were two decorated trees on either side of the door, and lights ran the length of the barn on both sides. On the right side, there was a fire where people could sit nearby and warm themselves. There was a huge lighted wreath on the door. The barn was the biggest one that Kathleen had ever seen. There was live music playing and carolers singing inside.

"What is this place, Frank?" she asked brusquely.

"It's a barn that is decorated really special for Christmas, and carolers singing Christmas songs and live music."

"I can't believe you would bring me to a barn!" she cried angrily.

Frank's head dropped, and his demeanor changed immediately. "I'm sorry, I thought…"

Then she broke out in a smile that lit up the inside of Frank's heart.

"Frank, I was kidding. I love this. I've never done anything like this before, and I'm all about new experiences. Frank, this is truly amazing, and I love the decorations, all the lights. The way they reflect off the snow. Everything's so beautiful."

"Oh, I'm so relieved. You scared me."

"I'm sorry, Frank."

"Are you ready to go in?" He looked at her, and his heart almost melted. She looked incredible. Amazing. Unforgettable.

"Yes, Frank. I'm ready," she whispered.

He studied her lips and wanted to kiss them so badly. She was so close to him. So warm, and it felt wonderful. Without thinking, he took his hand and touched her lips. She looked up at him. He slowly moved closer to her face. He could feel her warm breath. He drew closer and, raising his head a little, kissed her on her forehead.

She saw him looking at her lips. *Is he going to kiss me?* she wondered. She didn't move. She stopped breathing. She could feel his breath and wished he'd just kiss her. She wanted it. She was disappointed when he went for her forehead instead, but it made her tingle. Just that made her tingle. She wondered what it would feel like to have his lips on hers—to feel his embrace.

"Well, Kathy, shall we go inside?" he asked, breaking the spell. He got down and offered his hand to help her down.

Her shoes touched the ground. "I'm so ready to go inside."

He opened his arm, and she slipped her arm through it.

They walked through the door, and Kathleen couldn't believe what she was seeing.

There were decorated trees in every corner of the room. Garland hung from the rafters, and lights were strung all through it. Ribbon was strung on the walls in large curves all around the room. Massive lit wreaths were hung in four places. It was incredible, and she loved it.

There were three long tables pushed together with red-and-white plaid tablecloths for covering and one beautiful Christmas arrangement with greens, candles, and ribbon. Food of every variety had covered almost every other inch of the table, except for the plates, silverware, and napkins. There was punch—with glasses and a ladle with which to serve it. On the other side of the room, there was a booth to buy coffee and hot chocolate.

Frank studied her as she took it all in. She was overwhelmed with joy. He loved watching her.

There was a fiddler, guitarist, accordionist, and they had even procured a piano and pianist for the event. It was the biggest town celebration of the year and the most well attended. It seemed the whole town was there. People were walking around enjoying Christmas villages, decorations of every sort, and homemade items for sale. Joy surrounded them.

Frank looked at Kathleen and nodded. "Well, you want to look around before the carol singing starts?"

"There's a 'carol sing' that everyone can join?"

"I knew you would like that."

She could hardly contain the happiness she felt in this man's presence. He made her heart flip just looking at him.

"Would you like to look around a little?"

"I thought you'd never ask." Her face was glowing like a Christmas tree.

He placed his hand at the small of her back and led her to the side of the barn. The Christmas music was lively and fun. They stopped several times to buy ornaments she liked and a wreath that was beautifully made.

"Look at this angel," she said adoringly. "It's so beautiful."

"Not as beautiful as you, my dearest," he said as he wrapped his arm around her shoulder and kissed her on the cheek.

She blushed.

Twenty minutes later, Frank suggested that they eat something before they dropped from exhaustion. She enthusiastically agreed.

Frank loaded his plate with spoons full of casseroles, then headed for the brownies, pies, and Christmas cookies. His eyes danced, and there was music in his heart. He couldn't remember when he'd felt so good and so happy.

Kathleen laughed when she looked at his plate. "How long has it been since you've eaten, Frank, a week?"

"No, more like a month." He laughed. "Hey, I'm a growing boy, and a growing boy has to eat—and preferably something someone else cooked," he said with laughter showing in his eyes.

"Frank Atwood, if you grew anymore, you'd be a redwood tree!" They laughed together.

"Are you having fun, Kathy?" he asked softly enough that only she could hear.

"I'm having more fun than I can ever remember. This is something I will never forget!" They looked in each other's eyes and held that gaze for several seconds.

When they finished eating, they made their way back to the floor for more shopping and looking. Then the caroling started, and they sang together with the rest of the people. Too soon, they were announcing it would be their last song and time to leave.

Kathleen felt like she had entered a fairy tale with "and they lived happily ever after" for the ending. She truly hoped that would be the case.

When it ended, Frank found their coats and guided her outside to the sleigh waiting for them. He helped her up and then got up beside her. The driver snapped the reins, and the horse trotted off. It had stopped snowing, but the temperature was still below freezing.

Frank wrapped his arm around her shoulder and pulled the blanket over their laps.

She looked up to him. "Frank, if I'm dreaming, would you be so kind as to not wake me?" She breathed.

"My dearest Kathy, I'm in the same dream." He looked down and kissed her on the cheek. She rested her head on his shoulder. She had stopped talking, which for her was a Christmas miracle. He looked down at her and found she was fast asleep. He smiled. They stayed like that until they reached the truck.

When the sleigh stopped, it was next to the truck. Kathleen raised her head slowly.

"Oh, Frank. I'm so sorry. I must have fallen asleep."

"Yes, it was very rude for a first date," he said, teasing her.

She hit his shoulder, and he laughed. "Come on, let's get you home so you can fall sleep in your own bed," he said, although the last thing he wanted to do was put an end to this evening. He helped her down and up into the truck. She scooted closer to him and put her head back on his shoulder.

"What are you going to do? Fall asleep on me again?" He chuckled.

"No, I'm still a little chilly though."

"Okay, I'll turn on the heater, but it takes a while to warm up."

"Who needs a heater when I've got you?" she teased. "I don't want this night to end, Frank. It was a wonderful night. You were wonderful."

"Well, at some point, the night will end, whether we want it to or not, my dearest."

"Don't be so practical. I've loved being with you tonight. Can't we stay up and watch the sunrise together?"

"That would be great, but it's going to snow, so there won't be a sunrise." He smiled.

She hit his shoulder. "I told you to stop being so practical!"

"Ouch. Well, someone has to be," he said.

They pulled up in front of the house. He turned off the engine, and they sat looking at each other. He took a deep breath.

"Well, I think it's time I walked you to the door. Come on," he said as he got out of the truck and went around, opened her door, and helped her get down.

They walked quietly to the door, neither wanting it to end. When they were at the threshold, Frank took her slowly in his arms. Bending down to her face, he ran his finger down her neck and then traced her lips. He leaned closer, and her body leaned into his. He was so close to her lips, and then he stopped for a couple seconds and brushed his lips on hers. He looked up at her, as if to ask for permission, and then bent down and kissed her the way he had wanted to the whole evening. It was perfect. Better than he imagined.

She basked in the kiss. It was like a hundred violins started playing when his lips touched hers. She could have stayed that way forever. She didn't want him to leave—ever.

Franklin pushed back and took a deep breath. "Wow! That was one amazing kiss," he exclaimed. "Do you kiss all the boys like that?" He grinned.

"Would you believe me if I told you that was my first one?" she asked.

He chuckled. "No."

"It's true, Frank. I've always stayed away from boys and dating. I had more important things to do and didn't want to get involved."

"So, what changed?"

"You did. You've changed my mind about a lot of things."

"Kathy, I don't know if I should tell you this or not, but I'm going to. I'm crazy about you. I was married for almost twenty years, and I did love my wife, but I never felt about her the way I feel about you. I hope that doesn't scare you half to death, but it's the truth, as long as we're being honest with each other."

"My sweet Frank." She stepped closer to him and leaned into his body. "You don't scare me one bit. I've never been so happy or ever met anyone like you." She looked up to him and brushed her lips against his cheek. "Just don't get scared and run away from me, okay?" she pleaded, whispering.

"Not likely. I don't think I even could, Kathleen."

"Kathy."

"Whatever."

They both laughed.

"I think you better get inside so I can go home," he said lovingly.

"Frank," she whispered. "Kiss me one more time."

"Your wish is my command." He bent down and sweetly kissed her.

He took a deep breath. "Okay, let's get your little tuchus inside."

She smiled. She fished her keys out of her bag and handed them to Franklin. He unlocked the door, opened it, and she walked inside.

"May I call on you Friday? I can't promise an evening like this one…"

"As long as I'm with you, I don't care what we do," she said with stars in her eyes.

"Okay, then, I will see you on Friday." He turned and walked toward the pickup. She watched, hoping he would look back.

He turned around, smiling, and waved as he got into the truck and watched her close the door. He started the engine and drove off.

CHAPTER 34

It seemed like all he could think about were all those papers on the desk, and still no answers as to what to do about them. He'd been looking through them, reading every word to see if there was anything new he could see this time around. But he was so tired, and halfway through, he put his arms on the desk, and his head soon followed.

A knock on the door woke him with a start. Another knock. He tried to get the sleep out of his eyes while standing up and walking toward the door.

"I'm coming!" he shouted. "Hold your horses!" He opened the door to see Maddie standing there.

"Maddie, come in," he said as his face brightened.

"Thanks. I just haven't seen you for a couple of days and wondered if you were okay."

"Oh, I guess so. Just tired and so confused. Trying to put this puzzle together is making me borderline insane," he said with his head in his hands.

"Just borderline?" She smiled.

She sat on the chair by the fire, and Raff was on the couch. Maddie took a closer look. He did look tired. *All this weird stuff is getting to him*, she thought. *He looked down. Depressed even.*

"Maddie, would you come over and sit with me? I need you beside me right now."

"Oh, Raff, of course." She walked to the sofa, sat right beside him, and wrapped her arms around him. Raff squeezed her tight and didn't let go. He finally pulled back a little and faced her. "I love you, Maddie, so very much." He searched her eyes and found desire in them. He pulled her to him and stared in her eyes and then her lips. He placed his hand behind her hair and ran his fingers through it, and he drew closer to her face. He brought his lips to hers and kissed them lightly and put his head back up. Then bent down again and kissed her long and passionately.

Maddie pushed back and said, "Well, Mr. Mayfield, you sure know how to make a girl feel welcomed." She giggled.

Raff relaxed a little. "I guess I've been missing that, missing you. I've been stuck in this house trying to work but getting nowhere," he said, shaking his head. "I don't know what to do or where to turn."

"You need a break. You know what? There's nothing in this house that would bring you cheer or anything positive right now. It would drag the most joyful person down. We're going to get you out of this house and cut down a tree. You need some color and cheer in this house. Right now, it's just dark and dingy. Let's get you some fresh air, cut down a tree, and get some lights on it."

"I don't know. I really don't feel much like doing anything."

"Really. Do you want another kiss?"

"Do you even have to ask?"

"Well then, let's get your coat and boots on and get this place warmed and cheery."

"What about my kiss?"

"Not till we're done, cowboy," she toyed with him.

"Oh my goodness, you're blackmailing me for a kiss?" He chuckled.

"I prefer to call it a motivator. Is it working?"

"Yes, it most certainly is. Let's go and have a little fun."

They both dressed for the cold weather and raced out the door, down the stairs, and to the car. They laughed, and Raff could feel the cloud lifting he'd been carrying on his shoulders the past couple of days. This was something he'd needed, and Maddie knew it instinctively.

They brought back a short-needled pine tree and placed it in front of the window.

"You smell that tree. It's like bringing the outdoors indoors. Maybe it will get rid of some of the musty smell in here and will make you feel a whole lot better. And maybe instead of sitting in the office, we could bring a table in here where you can sit and work and enjoy the color of the tree. It will cheer you up. I guarantee it!"

"You know, that's not a bad idea. I would really like that."

"Raff, where did your folks put Christmas decorations?"

"We didn't have any."

"Okay, let's grab those coats again and head into town for some lights and inexpensive ornaments. We could go to the store and get some popcorn and cranberries and string them for a garland. Raff Mayfield, we are going to make this room something you can enjoy until after Christmas and keep you sane at the same time."

"While we're in town, how about a bowl of chili or chowder to warm our insides before we head home? How does that sound, my sweet?" Raff suggested.

"Sounds great. Let's get moving, cowboy. We've got a project to finish."

They headed to the General Store and bought lights, two boxes of ornaments, some popcorn and cranberries, and tinsel. Then some candles for the table and fireplace mantle. Raff was getting excited. He even decided to cut a couple boughs off the bottom of the tree to place on the mantle over the fireplace. He also knew where he could cut some holly to put on the boughs. The day that had started so somber and depressing, now felt exciting and fun. He really did need this break.

After the store, they headed toward the café for soup. Maddie ordered chili, and Raff took the clam chowder, and they split a ham sandwich. They enjoyed their time together, and Raff reminded her twice about the kiss to come just in case she'd forget.

They left the café and put all their Christmas decorations in the trunk and took off for home. Raff brought in the boxes into the house and sat them down by the tree.

They started with the colored lights and put two long strings on it. He loved the color it brought to the room. Maddie opened the ornament boxes and started placing them on the tree. By the time darkness had fallen, they were finished, except for the garland and icicles. The garland would have to come first, so they popped the corn and put the cranberries in a bowl, and both sat on the couch ready to poke a needle and thread through popcorn kernels and fresh cranberries.

After Raff had poked the needle in his finger several times, he turned to Maddie.

"Maddie, this is the most dangerous work I have ever done, and if I finish this without losing a finger, I deserve more than one kiss!" he said teasingly.

Maddie laughed. "Well, I guess maybe I could allow that. It seems like a pretty high price, though. I'll have to take it under advisement, you understand," she said all businesslike.

After placing on the tinsel, Raff placed the boughs on the mantle and added candles.

"It's beginning to look like Christmas in here, finally. It's really quite beautiful, isn't it, Raff?"

"It certainly is, and it does change a person's mood. And it smells so good in here, too. Now, I think I have a reward coming...if I'm not mistaken, my darlin'."

"You think so, huh?"

"I do, and if I don't get it immediately, I will tickle you first, to get your defenses down, then go for those amazing lips of yours. Either way, I'm getting those kisses. So, it's your play, what are you going to do? There's no place to run and no place to hide," he said, very amused.

"Well, sir, I'm not sure it's proper behavior being alone and all," she said demurely.

"Well, what's it gonna be?"

She was seated on the couch, and he ran and jumped in right beside her. He grabbed her and wrapped his arms around her and slowed down as he lowered his head and gave her a sweet kiss. The second one was longer, but he stayed away from the passionate kind for both their sakes.

"Mmm," she said with her eyes closed, savoring his lips and the closeness to his body. They fit together so well, and she was thankful for that. She wanted more, but she knew that when Raff pushed back, it was because he didn't want to go too far. She wanted that purity for herself and for him, too, so she was okay with that.

"Maddie, I'm really tired. It's been a very long day. I think I'm going to send you home, and I'm going to bed. I'm sorry to cut this a little short, but why don't you help me over here tomorrow, and we can maybe talk things through and discover something together. I don't seem to be getting anywhere on my own."

"Sounds fine, Raff."

"Maddie, thank you for getting me out of my funk. It means a lot to me."

"No problem. Anytime."

Raff walked her outside to her car and they stood by the driver's door.

"Thanks again, Maddie."

"I wouldn't mind a goodbye kiss, cowboy," she said, smiling.

"Oh really? I guess I could handle that." He walked up to her, and she leaned into him. She put her arms around his neck. He looked down and slowly dropped his head and kissed her on the forehead, then chuckled when he saw her irresistible frown of hers.

"Raff Mayfield, that does not qualify as a genuine kiss," she teased.

"Well, then, I guess you better state the rules beforehand from now on." He opened the car door for her and said good night, with a very large smile on his face, then laughed.

"See ya tomorrow, Maddie. I love you."

"Tomorrow, Mayfield."

She got into the car and drove off.

CHAPTER 35

Hettie was standing in the hall when Kathleen closed the door. Kathleen turned around and saw her there.

"Aaaaa!" she screamed. "Hettie, you scared me half to death! What are you doing here?" she asked.

"Do ya realize it's 1:04 a.m.? That's over an hour past midnight. Kathleen! Where have ya been?" she asked angrily. She saw the startled look on Kathleen's face and roared with laughter.

"Did ya have a good time, sweetheart?" she asked softly.

"Oh, Hettie, it was a dream. I've never been so happy. He's an amazing man!" She said dreamily.

"You're in love with him, ain't ya?"

"All I know is how I feel when I'm with him. He's so good to me, and sweet, funny, kind, and so very handsome!"

"Ya might wanna take your time to get to know him better," she warned.

"Hettie, I'm forty-five years old. How much time do I have? I think Frank and I are old enough to know our own minds," she said thoughtfully.

"Guess that's true 'nough. Jes' so good to see ya fin'lly happy. I've known ya my whole life and purtty much raised ya. I love ya like you're my own daughter, and I've been waitin' for this for years. I'm so happy for ya, honey."

Kathleen wrapped her arms around her and gave her the biggest hug ever.

123

"I love you, too. You pretty much have been my mother, especially after she died." Kathleen looked around. "Hettie, can you do me a favor? After seeing decorations everywhere inside and outside that barn tonight, I realized we haven't done anything here yet."

"Barn? Bet there's a story there I wanna hear later."

"Can we have the gardeners cut down a tree or go to a tree lot and get a tree for every room and one for each of the staff's rooms and yours and mine, of course, and a huge one for the large parlor. And if we don't have enough ornaments to decorate with, order them and have a couple of the men pick them up. Can we do that?"

"Kathleen, that's a lotta trees."

"Okay, just the rooms we use the most then, plus the staff's rooms and ours. Is that better?"

"A little, but who's going to decorate all those trees?"

"I don't know. Can we at least work on it? And save the big one for Frank and me to decorate. Oh, and string lights outside the house, and light the trees that are close to the house," she said, her face glowing.

"My, oh my, ya got it bad, huh?"

"It's Christmas! The time for joy and miracles! It's Jesus's birthday! Let's celebrate!" she cried joyfully while twirling.

"Wow!" Hettie said, shaking her head. "Lord have mercy, this girl is plum crazy in love."

CHAPTER 36

F ranklin sat in his rocker as the memories of this evening rolled over him. He couldn't be more pleased. He was head over heels in love with her, and she was pretty close to that, if not there already. What a time they had. It was like one of those romantic movies but not in black and white. This was in living, breathing color. Color was everywhere. On her cheeks, on her lips, in her eyes, her hair. Yes, he loved her. He could almost feel guilty about the differences in the loves between Pearly and Kathleen, but he knew that everyone is different and so is love. It means different things to different people. But he had never felt like this before.

Every thought had her in it. Her laugh, the way she moved her little tuchus, the way she smiled, talked—everything about her. He knew they hadn't been together long, but he'd fallen in love with her the first time they bumped into each other—slowly at first. But then it was like a snowball, rolling down a hill, picking up speed, and gathering more snow as it fell. Here, it'd been just two weeks later, and he was even considering marrying her. Would she think it too soon? The kisses tonight. They were like heaven, and he wanted more. He could still feel them on his lips.

Yes, she's wealthy, but she liked him and knew he wasn't, so it must be okay. To be honest, he wasn't quite sure he could live in that fancy house. Not certain he could be comfortable there. On the other hand, he'd do almost anything to be with her; maybe that included a big move in the future. Maybe not. Maybe she wouldn't want to marry him at all. And on that one depressing note, he decided to go to bed. He walked to the bedroom, undressed, and got into bed. The sheets were cold, at first, but if he stayed still, it would warm up.

They were outside the estate and walking around the gardens. It was snowing lightly, and Franklin had his arm around Kathleen's shoulders. It was so quiet and beautiful. Franklin dropped his arm as they approached the door. Something hit him in the back. He turned and saw Kathleen pelt him in the back with a snowball.

Laughing, she threw another one. Missed.

"Oh, so you want to play, huh? You do know I was in a snow-ball-throwing contest a few years ago and won the championship. So, little girl, watch out!" He bent down, quickly made a snowball, and threw it at her. It hit her shoulder. He bent down to make another, when one flew past his ear.

She laughed and pointed at him.

"Missed me." He threw another and lightly hit her back as she was bending to make another.

"Okay." He quickly limped to her and grabbed her. "Truce," he said, laughing. He held her arms.

They stopped and stared into each other's eyes. He put his arms around her and drew her in and kissed her with all the love he possessed.

"Kathy, I know it's only been weeks since we met, but I'm so in love with you, I can't have a thought that you aren't a part of. I can't imagine my life without you in it, wherever that may be. I promise to love you, to support you, to laugh with you and cry with you. I promise I will always be faithful to you. Please, will you do me the honor of being my wife?"

She studied him with a smile on her lips and kissed him softly.

"Is that a yes or a no, my dearest?"

"That is a…"

He woke with a jerk.

CHAPTER 37

Driving home from work, Miles rehearsed the conversation he'd had with Raff. Thankful that he'd seen him grow up into a seemingly responsible young man, especially since he apologized to him after all these years. It was a good call on his part, and he was glad. The one thing concerning him was about Raff's dad's prescriptions. It just sounded fishy. He'd decided he would do a little detective work, but not without asking Raff's permission. It wasn't too late and thought maybe he'd just drop by his house and talk to him about it. He didn't think Raff would have a problem with him being there without an invitation. The more he thought of it, the more he thought it was the right thing to do.

He pulled in his driveway, walked up the stairs, and knocked on the door.

Raff opened the door expecting it to be Maddie, because she's the only one that had been to his house in some time.

"Mad—Mr. Strattford," he said with surprise. "Um, come in, please."

Raff motioned him toward the couch in the front room, and Miles walked in and sat down.

"Wow! That's some tree you got there," he said, staring at the tree. "The mantel looks beautiful, too," he said with surprise.

"Thanks, Mr. Strattford. My girlfriend and I did it yesterday. I'm really enjoying it. You know, it's my very first Christmas tree. We didn't celebrate Christmas when I was growing up," he said sadly.

"I'm sorry, I didn't know that. Must have been difficult," he acknowledged.

His brow furrowed. "It was, but I got used to it. It wasn't until I gave my life to God that everything changed. I wanted to celebrate Christmas, so Maddie and I decorated her house, and last night, we did mine. Getting to know him has made the most wonderful change in my life."

"That's nice, Raff. Real nice. The fact that you apologized to me showed a change I was never expecting. So that's good," Miles said, affirming Raff's decision.

"Well, thanks, but I needed to. And I wanted to thank you for your forgiveness. I didn't deserve it."

"No one does. That's why it's so powerful. Forgiveness is one of the highest virtues we can experience. So please, don't give it another thought. Raff, I wanted to ask you something."

"Okay."

"Would you mind if I did a little detective work regarding that prescription of your dad's? I have some sources I can check with, if that's okay with you."

"Oh, that would be great," he said with relief. "I would really appreciate it. I feel so overwhelmed with all that I have to do to with Dad's...stuff, that it would be a relief for me. It's so kind of you to offer. Thank you," he said gratefully.

"Raff, I know a little of your background and I know you had a rough go of it. So, if there's anything else I can do to help, I would be happy to. I have plenty of time—just my job, otherwise free."

"Thank you, I just might ask for help, if you're sure."

"I am. Can you bring me all his prescriptions?" he asked. "They could be useful."

"Sure, I'll be right back." He stood and walked to the bathroom and took the prescriptions. He was walking into the living room when he saw Miles studying the tree. He touched the tinsel and smiled. It even seemed like his eyes lit up a little. Raff hadn't seen Mr. Strattford smile very often, so he took note of it. He walked in the room and took the bottles to Mr. Strattford.

"Got a Christmas tree at your house, Mr. Strattford?"

"No. I don't usually decorate for Christmas. Just not my thing, I guess," he said, looking down.

"I see. Well, who knows, you might change your mind someday."

He tilted his head and shrugged his shoulders. "I doubt it. Well, thank you for the prescriptions, I'd best be getting home. I'll let you know if I find anything that might help you. And, if there is anything else, you know how to reach me." He stood up and walked toward the door.

"Thank you so much for doing this for me. It's a godsend, really." Raff stood, went to the door, and shook his hand, thanking him again for his offer. He opened the door, and Mr. Strattford left.

CHAPTER 38

Sitting in the living room drinking coffee, Raff filled Maddie in on the visit with Mr. Strattford.

"He told me that he would take the prescription bottles and do a little detective work to see if he could find any new information about it. He has people he can talk to that we can't. He also offered to help with anything else we needed. He thought he might have a different perspective than we would."

"That's great, Raff. After all this time and the history you had with him, that's pretty incredible," she said, surprised.

Seconds passed as Maddie was trying to organize her thoughts.

"Raff, I've been thinking," she said hesitantly. "This may sound way off base, but try to follow me and see if it makes any sense to you at all."

"Okay, go ahead."

"What if the debt and the drugs are connected somehow? What if…maybe that skeleton key has the answer to all of it?"

"How would they be connected?"

"I'm not sure. But think about it. It doesn't make sense that your dad not only didn't pay his debt but left all the papers on his desk out in the open. Then there's the bookcase filled with all the cash he could possibly want in the form of those books. There's just something not right about it. Something's off."

"Okay, but why would anyone want to kill my dad? Was he a threat to someone? Did he hurt somebody, and this was a revengeful act?" he asked.

"I don't know yet, but I think we need to find out what that key opens. I think that has the answers—not Lucas Sprat. Oh, and thinking about him, just what was the paper he wanted you to sign, and why was he so eager to have you do it?"

"I don't know. So, you think he's got something to do with it?"

She shrugged. "Don't know, but if you're game, why don't we start looking in the attic? We'll turn this house upside down until we find it!"

"Okay, let the scavenger hunt begin!" he said with renewed positivity.

"Sounds good. Where's the key? We should probably take it up with us."

"Yeah, I got it in my pocket."

"Okay, let's get this done."

Raff reached the top step with Maddie close behind. He approached the attic with dread in his heart, praying that God would give them the wisdom to find what they needed.

They glanced around the room, looked at each other, and sighed. Raff hung his head and immediately felt defeated.

In the corner by the window was unevenly stacked furniture of every variety. A chest and chairs, table, framed pictures, and more. An old mattress was on the floor, with boxes of every size; a cradle and rocking horse were sitting on top. At least an inch of dust and scattered papers were just a part of the inventory on the floor. Cobwebs seemed to grace every inch of the rafters, and some hung all the way to the floor. There was a naked light bulb in the middle of the room with a pull chain, and the one window was so dirty it was almost impossible to see through, but it still offered a sliver of light.

It was a mess, and if it weren't so important, Raff would have turned right back around and gone downstairs, never to walk up the stairs again. But there was too much riding on it. He had to find whatever it was that key opened. He was hoping that had the answer to the mystery.

Raff went over to a box and began looking through it. Grocery lists, parts of old letters, a glass snowman ornament, and old sheets. "Nothin' here."

Maddie opened a big chest that had so much dust on it she couldn't see what the decoration was on it. She rifled through what was on the inside. Blankets, a very old, broken clock, papers that meant nothing, and then she saw a small box. It was blue-flowered toile on a white background and about 8"x6". She opened it.

There was an old high school graduation program, an old corsage, probably from a high school prom, a rhinestone hair clip, and a letter. The letter was addressed to Olivia from George. She opened the envelope, feeling a little guilty, but not enough to put it back without reading it. She knew it was private, but they were looking for answers, after all.

She began to read:

Dear Olivia,

I was wondering if I could walk you home after school. I could get you home on time so your dad doesn't get mad. I like talking with you and spending time with you. If you want to, please meet me at the library after the last bell.

Your friend,
George

"Raff, you should come and see this. It's quite interesting."

"Okay." He walked over and sat down beside her. "What is it?"

"It's a note written to your mom from your dad way back in high school."

"Really?" He read it. "Wow, it sounds like they were starting to date. That's so weird."

"Why? Your dad couldn't have come out of the womb mean and cantankerous."

"You didn't know my dad." They laughed.

"I'm sure there's some kind of a love story. She saved a corsage from back then. I think it was from your dad."

"It is interesting. I wasn't sure he knew how to love."

Maddie's brow raised. "I thought you forgave your father."

"I did, but that doesn't mean I can forget everything. I mean, I guess maybe that stuff comes back up, and sometimes it's easy to get back in the same thinking pattern I used to have."

"Raff, that happens to all of us. It's Satan trying to get at you. Trying to get you back into old thought processes that make you so miserable. He is the great deceiver. That's what he does. His goal is to get you to walk away from God and go back to your old ways. Then you've lost your Christian testimony to all those people you've already talked to about how God has changed your life. Why Christmas means so much to you now."

"Wow. I didn't know that. I'm so glad you're here to help me through stuff like this, because I have so much to learn."

"We all do. Don't get down on yourself, but next time, maybe you'll remember where all those thoughts come from. They're not from God, and that's where you always need to turn for everything."

"Thanks. I haven't read the Bible the last few days, so I need to get back to that."

"It happens. We get busy, then it's easy to eliminate that from our schedule. I haven't known a Christian yet that hasn't struggled with that.

"Let's get out of here. I'm ready to go play—maybe see a movie or something. What do you say, cowboy? How about a romantic comedy?"

"You mean a chick flick? How about a World War II movie instead?"

"I think I'd like a little romance."

"We just saw *Gone with the Wind*, it doesn't get any more romantic than that."

"Yeah, but *Gone with the Wind* didn't end happily."

"World War II did. We won."

"But there's no romance."

"Have you ever been to a movie that didn't have a woman in it somewhere? Even in the middle of a war?"

She sighed. "True, but it's not the same."

"Okay, here's the deal. I'll take you out for Italian, then at the theater, I'll buy you the biggest bag of popcorn you can possibly eat, and if you want more, I'll get up in the middle of the movie and buy you another bag. How's that?"

"Milk Duds, too?"

"Good grief, woman. Don't you ever get full?"

"Yeah, but when you're at a movie, you eat movie food. Them's the rules, Mayfield. Take it or leave it."

"Man, you drive a hard bargain. Fine. You win."

"Cowboy, you ain't seen nothin' yet!"

CHAPTER 39

It was Friday evening as Franklin drove up the driveway to the estate. He couldn't believe what he saw. There were Christmas lights strung all over the house. There were lights around the windows and doors. There were wreaths hung on both sides of the front door, and all the trees and shrubbery were lit with an enormous amount of color. Franklin's jaw dropped. It had just been two days since he had been here, and this was truly amazing. He wondered how many staff people it took to accomplish such an effort. It was stunning!

He strode to the door and knocked. Hettie opened the door.

"Well, Mr. Frank, please come in. Kathleen will be right down," she said with a little chuckle.

"Franklin. Thank you, Mrs...."

She ignored his comment. Gesturing him inside, she shut the door. She ushered him into the large parlor and asked him to sit down.

"Hettie, Frank. Just Hettie."

"Thank you, Hettie," he said a little awkwardly.

She offered to take his coat, and since he didn't know how long Kathleen would be, he humored her. Hettie showed him inside to the large parlor.

Trying to take in the room, he first noticed the huge Christmas tree in the bay window. It must be at least twelve feet tall. It was undecorated, but he'd already seen down the hall to the other open rooms to know there were more that were decorated. He was floored. He couldn't imagine how this could have happened so quickly, but it was beautiful, and he was thoroughly enjoying it. It made him think of his cabin and how bare it looked in comparison. He shook his head. His eyes circled the room. There was wallpaper on the walls that had a white background and small pink and shimmering, white flowers with a tiny pink stripe separating the rows. On the floor was another Persian rug that had a red border and was floral inside with pinks and reds. It complemented everything. He like this round-shaped room with a beautiful chandelier in the center.

Kathleen entered the room, and Frank's face lit up like a lighthouse. She smiled and walked right over to him, throwing her arms around him, and hugged him tightly.

"Frank, I missed you so much. It's so good to see you," she said, beaming and excited.

Franklin thought he'd never seen anything so beautiful—not even the Christmas trees.

"Hello, my dearest, I've missed you too." He was hardly able to contain the joy he felt. He kissed her on the forehead and put his hand in her hair.

"So, shall we get our coats and go?" he asked.

"Ah…ah, Frank, I hope you don't mind, but I wondered if we could have dinner here and maybe decorate this tree together. I saved it just for us," she said, smiling. "I mean, if that doesn't mess up your plans too much."

"Well, I guess it's okay. I didn't have anything big planned." He was wondering how he fit in to this place, and if he would ever be comfortable tonight.

She could see in his eyes that he was anxious in his surroundings and had instructed Hettie not to make anything for dinner that would be too "fancy." She settled on filet mignon with baked red potatoes and whatever vegetable Hettie decided. Dessert would be apple pie with vanilla ice cream. Simple and food Franklin would enjoy. She looked at him as she watched him peruse the room.

"Frank, I know you feel a bit uncomfortable with all this…" She moved her arm around the room. "I don't know how to change it for you, but please understand that you mean everything to me, and if you would rather leave and do something else, I totally understand," she said, sympathizing.

"Kathy, yes, this is a little overwhelming, but if you can feel comfortable in my pickup, I guess I can try to adapt to your world," he said, smiling. "But don't get upset if I start staring at things. I've never seen anything like this before. I do like this room, though. It's relaxing. The couch is a nice size, great for cuddling. Wanna try?" he asked teasingly.

She looked at him, searching his eyes, and loved him more than she ever thought possible. How did she get so lucky? No, not lucky, only God could have put these two people together who were so different in lifestyles, but not so different in heart.

"Frank, how would you feel about eating at the table in the kitchen?" she asked, trying to quell his anxiety.

"I would like that very much, thank you." Relief washed over his face.

Frank finally relaxed when his steak and the rest of his meal was plated. The kitchen felt a lot more like home, even though it had the most up-to-date appliances. There was no wallpaper at all in the kitchen. Painted white from the ceiling midway down and then finished in an emerald green to the floor. The table was a custom-built, dark-brown, wooden, rectangular, and probably sat as many as six people comfortably, with a large throw rug underneath in beige. The kitchen counter was butcher block with a different color wood for each strip and ran the length of the room, only interrupted by a large white sink and with a window looking out onto the beautiful gardens. It was something. There was a small oak table used for a worktable, and a large pantry behind it all enclosed. He was sure Hettie knew where everything was and nothing ever out of place. And probably filled each shelf with anything and everything imaginable.

"Well, Mr. Frank, Kathleen tells me ya took her to a barn for a date. I know there's a good story there that I wanna hear," she said, laughing.

"Okay, Hettie. I give up. I see you'll never call me Franklin. You're as stubborn as Kathy is. So, please, call me Frank," he said, teasing.

Hettie laughed. "You're right, Frank, about the name, but not the stubborn part. That title belongs to Kathleen alone. World record holder, I think." She laughed.

"Will you please stop talking about me like I'm not in the room?"

They all laughed. The conversation was light and enjoyable. So much so that Franklin almost forgot where he was.

After dinner, Kathleen led Franklin into the big parlor to decorate the tree.

"I guess we better get to it. It's going to take a while. I haven't seen a tree so big in anyone's house before." Truthfully, he hadn't been to that many homes, and certainly none like this one.

Franklin took the box of lights and strung twelve strings on the tree. Kathy and he put up all the ornaments. There were no homemade ones, only store-bought ones, but they were very beautiful, and there were so many different kinds. They put up several silver garlands.

They both stood back and looked. "Okay, Kathy, I think it's time to plug in those lights."

"Let's do a countdown."

"Okay. Three, two, one. Plug them in!"

The tree lit up, and it was well worth the wait.

"Isn't it beautiful, Frank?"

"Yes, it is. We make a good team, my dearest."

"We do indeed."

They both enjoyed it so much, until Franklin took a glance at the time.

"Oh, my goodness, it's time for me to go, Kathy. It's almost midnight."

"Frank, I really wish you didn't have to."

"Me too."

"Will you at least please kiss me goodbye?"

"Try and keep me away." He took her in his arms and kissed her passionately.

"Kathy, I wish I could tell you what's in my heart, but I just don't think you're ready to hear it yet."

"You'd be surprised what I'm ready for, Frank. Tell me, please?"

"Are you sure?"

"Quite sure."

"Once I say it, I can't take it back."

"Please, Frank, say it."

"I love you, Kathy. With all my heart and soul. Every thought is of you. You're funny and smart, and beautiful—so beautiful. You're not afraid of saying what you think and give an opinion on just about anything."

"You're so right about the funny and beautiful part. Go on."

Franklin laughed. "You just proved my point. I promise to support you, to care for you…"

"Frank…"

"Please let me finish."

"But, Frank…"

"Kathy, please."

"Frank, I know, but…"

"Kathleen Brennan, will you please stop talking and let me finish."

"Okay, but…"

"I'll take care of you when you're sick, and when we argue…"

"Frank…"

"Okay, it's obvious that I can't keep you quiet, so I'm just going to say it. Marry me, Kathy. I've never loved anyone the way I love you."

"Frankie, I've been trying to say yes all along, but you wouldn't let me."

"Frankie? Okay, that's where I draw the line. From Franklin to Frank and now Frankie. I don't think so."

"If I call you that when we're alone, can I squeak it by you, and then kiss you?" she asked with a pout.

"I don't know, I can probably guarantee you that you can get just about anything you want with that cute little pouty thing you do. It's totally unfair. Cheating really."

"Now that's information a girl can use. Men have all the advantages, you know."

"Don't think so. There's that 'feminine wiles' thing going on that women do."

"Feminine wiles thing, huh?"

"Yes, and there must be a substantial punishment for a slippage of the tongue in public. And it will be brutal!"

"Brutal, huh, should I be worried?" she asked, smiling.

"Yes, very worried."

"What is it?"

"A whole week without a kiss. You think you can handle that?"

"Frank, you wouldn't!" Her jaw dropped. "A week, I can hardly last two minutes without a kiss when I'm with you."

"Can you do that?"

"Yes, I think so, because you could never last a week!"

"You're right about that. Okay, but I want to go on record as saying this better not ever be said in public."

"Yes, Frankie," she said, teasing. She walked over to him and kissed him on the cheek.

He rolled his eyes at her, and she laughed.

"See? Unfair. Now you're using kisses. Cheater."

Three seconds later.

"Wait! Did you say yes…that you'll marry me?"

"Yes, yes, of course, I'll marry you," she said, laughing. "I love you, Frankie."

"When, when do you want to?"

"How about Christmas Eve?"

"That far away, huh?"

"I don't want to wait, Frank. I want to be your wife and love you completely," she said with a shyness he found irresistible.

Frank's demeanor changed. "I don't know, I think maybe we should wait a couple years at least," he said, chuckling.

Kathleen punched him in the shoulder.

"Ouch!"

He picked her up in his arms. "Kathy, you just made me the happiest man alive. I love you so very much," he said and kissed her fervently. Then he lifted his head and searched her eyes. Lowering his head again, he kissed her longer, then lifted his head and put her down. He took a deep breath and blew it out.

"Okay, I better go. No more of those tonight. I only have to wait two weeks. It'll be the longest two weeks of my life," he said as he picked up his coat and walked toward the door. He turned back and said, "I love you," and then walked out the door.

Kathleen laughed as she twirled around several times. "I'm getting married!" she yelled.

Hettie was watching the whole thing. "My, oh my! Two weeks. Better get to plannin' this shindig. The two of them are so in love they don't know what to do. The one thing they got down pat is smoochin'." She laughed as she walked away.

CHAPTER 40

I n his rocker, Franklin lit his pipe and inhaled, sat back and relaxed. He let the day wash over him like a wave and reveled in the excitement of it all. He still couldn't believe he asked her, and he really couldn't believe that she said yes. *The most beautiful woman in the world wants me to be her husband. Wow!* he thought. He didn't know how there would ever be another thought in his head for the next two weeks!

Suddenly out of nowhere, uncertainty gripped him. *What if it's too soon? What if we really need more time to get to know each other? What if the differences will eventually tear us apart? She's never had a boyfriend before…maybe this is just a crush, an infatuation. Maybe it's just the romance that changed her feelings about me…*he worried.

I remember Pearly saying that all our days are numbered by God, so how do we know just how many we really have? Shouldn't I take advantage of every day I have left on this earth? Isn't that something the Bible said? He reasoned. At least it sounded familiar, somehow.

Franklin shook his head. The doubts encircled him and swiped and clawed at him, tearing him apart. He dropped his head in his hands. "What have I done?" There were tears, which while not foreign, were scarce, and uncomfortable. Devastated at the possibilities for disaster, and wounded beyond imagination, he considered what he should do.

He loved Kathleen far beyond anything he ever thought possible. But did she love him the same way? Was what she was feeling real or just a dream of a first love? She'd never been in love before, and maybe she was just in love with the idea of being in love. A chill went through his heart like a knife, wounding his very soul.

"Oh, God, how can I know for sure that this is a love that will last a lifetime?" he cried out. The questions and doubts were destroying everything that made the relationship so special—so wonderfully different and easy and positive and pure and delightful and hopeful and full-throttled, pedal-to-the-metal, run-for-the-goalposts fantastic! No, he loved this woman with a fulfilling and lasting love. And in his heart, he knew she loved him the same way. This was a "once you know it, you know it" kind of love. No doubts! No more questions. He would marry his love in two weeks, and they would love and grow together, no matter where that was, and be happily married for as long as they both lived. With that, he snuffed out his pipe, placed it on the table, and went to bed. He fell into a dreamless, deep sleep.

CHAPTER 41

The attic was still upstairs, and all the work they had to do was still in front of them. The scope of the search weighed on Raff, and it was easy to be discouraged. *What if we don't find anything that would unravel Dad's mysterious behavior?* he wondered. Maddie and he weren't Holmes and Watson, and yet that's exactly what they had to be to put these pieces together. "I hate puzzles! Never were my forte." His frustration level rose. He took a breath. "Calm down, Raff," he said under his breath.

But this puzzle had to come together, or he would lose the farm. He was glad it was winter, with snow and ice still inches thick, because it meant he didn't have to do any work on the apple orchard. Caring for that along with working on this other headache would be more than he could handle.

He was grateful that Maddie was not just willing to work with him on this, but was wanting to help. It made it easier and not quite so burdensome. It gave him someone with whom to bounce off ideas, talking through different scenarios, and the fact that he was in love with this "helper" didn't hurt either. It was tangible, touchable support; and to have Mr. Strattford working on the prescription thing was a massive relief. He didn't want to go to the police until he had something more concrete.

Pouring himself a second cup of coffee, he walked into the living room and sat in the chair next to the roaring fire that he'd started earlier. Sitting down, he placed his coffee on the table next to him. He began to pray aloud.

"Lord, I'm tired of this mess, but I know I have to straighten it out. I don't know how to do that, and I need your help. Please give Maddie and me wisdom and help in finding what we need. You know what that is, and where it is, would you please share it with us? In the meantime, I want to thank you again for Maddie and the love you've given us for each other. Please help me preserve her innocence, and for the first time in my life, because of you, I feel different about my own body. A sense that you want the same for me. I believe in your strength, and I ask for it now. Amen."

The knock on the door interrupted his thoughts. He walked to the door, opened it, and asked Maddie to come in.

"I just poured myself a cup of coffee, would you like one?"

"Sure," she said as she took off her coat and boots, threw her coat over the couch, and left her boots on the inside doormat. "I would love one," she said, seating herself on the couch.

"I'll be right back." He turned toward the kitchen and returned in seconds with her coffee in hand and placed it on the side table next to her. Sitting down next to her, he gave her a peck on the cheek.

"Maddie, thank you so much for helping me with this. You don't know what a relief it is to have someone here so I don't have to do this alone. I couldn't do this without you."

"Yes, you could, Raff. God would help you through it. That's what he does."

"It's funny you should say that, because I was just praying about that very thing, along with some other things," he said, smiling.

Tilting her head, she raised an eyebrow. "Okay, cowboy, what are you up to?" she asked suspiciously.

"Nothing," he said, chuckling, "I was just thanking God for you and the love we have for each other." Speaking of, he lowered his head and pulled her into a kiss. The kiss was sweet and wonderful.

"Okay, let's finish our coffee and then tackle that daunting attic, before I turn tail and run out of this house," he said, walking back to his chair and taking a sip of coffee.

"Yeah, I'm going back to the chest and see what else I can find there. It's been pretty interesting so far. Your mom saved that stuff from high school. That's a long time to hang on to something, so it obviously meant something to her."

"Finished with your coffee, my sweet? C'mon, let's go," he said in resignation.

They found their way to the attic again. Raff opened another box, not really in the mood to deal with it. But that's what he always did: run away when things got difficult. Never wanting to tackle the hard stuff. Now, he was forced to and didn't like it. He realized again that he let his mood interfere with what he knew to be the truth. That he wasn't doing this alone. God was with him, and he had prayed for wisdom earlier, and Maddie was here. He had to be patient and just go through the steps one at a time and try not to get overwhelmed.

"Nothin' here," he said after he finished going through the first box.

Maddie studied the chest. She really hadn't looked closely at it before. It was beautiful, minus the dust. The lid was rounded and had gold filigree all over it. There were handles encased in gold on both ends, and all around the bottom were hand-painted pictures of the skyline of New York City, including people down on the sidewalks, and it was probably fifty years old. This was not any ordinary chest, this was art! She blew off the dust and traced the filigree with her hand. *Wow!* she thought. *How would his family get something like this? This is an expensive chest.*

"Raff, have you ever seen this chest before?"

"No, why?"

"Because this is no ordinary chest. This thing costs a fortune all on its own."

"Great, another mystery, more questions."

"Come and look, you got to see this thing, it's beautiful," she said in awe.

Raff knelt beside her. "You're right, this is beautiful. I wonder how Dad got this?" An idea hit him. "You know, that might ease my money issues until we can figure this out. I've pretty much blown through my savings. Maybe this would pay off the debt and give me some breathing room. It is amazing, but I don't need it, and I've already decided to hang on to the books, so, that might be a way out and give me some cash to live on in the meantime."

"Would you really do that? I mean, it's beautiful. It might be worth keeping," she said thoughtfully.

"I have no more savings, and my time is running short to keep the farm. I don't have time to get a job. I'm kind of under the gun. Where else am I going to find the money to do this?" he asked, pleading with her. "What do you think? I'm open to suggestions. This would solve my immediate problems and give me the time I need to solve this riddle."

"I get it, I do." Seconds passed. "Ah, I have some money I've saved from the bookstore. I don't mind giving that to you."

Maddie loved her job. She was the manager of the Mountain View Bookstore in town. Since it was the only one, they did get a lot of customers, and especially around the holidays. She loved getting to know the customers, many of whom were repeaters. One she had become fairly close friends with was Kathleen. Even though she was much older, they really enjoyed each other's company and even went out to lunch on occasion. They shared their lives, books they loved, and loves they hoped someday may be relationships that lasted a lifetime.

"Maddie, I'm not taking your money! That's about the last thing I want to do. It's yours, and you earned it. You need it to live on. I blew everything I earned because of my…well, you know," he said ashamedly, "so I brought very little with me. I've almost exhausted everything."

"If you decide to do that, I'll support you. I understand." She nodded. "Let's get back to work," she said flatly.

He left her side and walked across the room and opened the next box. He sighed, looked up, and stared at her. He shook his head. *I have to think things through further, and I can't take it out on Maddie. It's not fair, and I don't want to hurt her*, he thought, chiding himself.

Maddie opened the chest and started rifling through it. She found an old Bible with a name on it. It belonged to Raff's mother.

"Raff, I just found your mom's Bible." She took it out and laid it on a nearby chair.

"That'll be fun to read her notes and stuff," he said as he crossed the room, picked it up, and leafed through it. "I'll take it downstairs when I go down. That's great!"

She took out blankets, old cards, an envelope with a name on it. She picked it up and read the name written on the envelope.

"Raff, you need to come and see this."

"What now, Maddie?" he said, irritated.

"Just drop what you're doing, and come over here!" She raised her voice, which told him she meant business. He recognized that tone from years ago. Once that tone was used, he knew not to mess with her.

"All right. I'm coming," he said with a smile in his voice, from the warm memories that had just run through his mind.

He knelt beside her again. "Look, I'm sorry I snapped at you. I didn't mean it."

"Nothing to worry about." She handed him the envelope.

"What's this?"

"It's an envelope with your name on it."

Raff looked at it, and his eyes widened.

"This is my dad's handwriting. I'd recognize it anywhere. But there's no address or anything."

"Think about it. No one knew where you were or when or if you were coming home. What else could he do?" she asked softly.

He shook his head and then let it drop. "Of course, you're right. I can't blame him for something that's my fault. I'm just so ashamed of my behavior, Maddie," he said, painfully.

"Forget all that, and read what he has to say. It must have been important to him to do this and then put it somewhere where he knew you would eventually find it."

"Maddie, I don't know if I want to read it. To be honest, I'm a little afraid of what's in it," he said hesitantly.

"You'll never know if you don't read it. I'm going to leave you alone and give you some space." She started to walk away.

"No." He grabbed her arm. "I don't want to be alone. Please stay with me. I need you here, and besides, I don't want to keep any secrets from you. I want an honest relationship. I think real love deserves it. I see couples who don't do this, and the results are not good. I want the closeness between us now to last forever. So please. Stay with me," he pleaded.

"Okay, if you're sure."

"I'm sure."

He began reading the letter.

> October 13, 1950
> Dear Raff,
>
> If you're reading this and I didn't hand it to you, then I'm gone. I didn't write this because I'm making excuses for myself, I wrote this because when you've read the whole letter, I hope you'll be able to forgive me.

Raff looked up at Maddie, and tears started to pool in his eyes.

> I started having chest pains and over the last two to three weeks they have gotten worse, so I assume that's what caused my death. The newest medication I got hasn't seemed to help. I don't know, maybe I read it wrong and took too many or not enough. But I took more over the last few days and the pain has gotten worse. So, I know I don't have much time left. I didn't want to go to Jesus and your mother without setting things straight with you.

He looked up again. "He's the last person I thought would go to Jesus. What happened?"

"Raff?"

"Oh, he said something about not wanting to go to Jesus until he set things straight with me."

"That's wonderful. This is what you needed to know."

He continued reading.

> We never could communicate well, but it was all my fault, not yours. I never let you work toward your strengths and what you wanted to do. I thought woodworking and being a mechanic were not career moves, which is why I wanted you to go to college. I wanted you to be a better man than I was. I thought the way to do that was to go and get a college degree. I was wrong. Later, I saw people who made a good living at making furniture and I kept hoping you would come home so I could tell you that.

"What is it? What's wrong?"

"I think he's trying to apologize to me."

"Are you okay?"

"I think so." He read on.

> I finally realized that you didn't even enjoy school and anything you did with your hands is where you excelled and were happy. I wished I'd understood that earlier. I misunderstood you, Raff, and I'm so very sorry.

Tears started down his cheeks. Maddie just watched, not wanting to interrupt him.

He continued.

> After your mother died, I found her Bible, and for some reason, which I understand now to be God, I started reading it. Hours at a time. I

wrote down my questions and went to talk with Pastor Ryan who worked with me and answered my questions with endless patience, and just a couple years ago, on Christmas Eve, I gave my life to Jesus and became a new person. I went to Bible study and learned how horribly I treated you and your mother. I wish now that I could go back and change everything, but I can't. But I can tell you how much I regret it, and how very sorry I am for all of it.

I love you, Raff, and always have. I just didn't know how to tell you or show it. I thought it a sign of weakness in men, so I avoided it. I couldn't show my real feelings.

My one wish after becoming a Christian, was that I could spend one more Christmas with you and your mother. I would do it differently now. Decorating the house, the Christmas tree… I wronged you there as well. I realize now that Christmas is the most meaningful of all the holidays because of God's gift of Jesus to us. So, no matter what time of year it is when you read this, I want to wish you a very Merry Christmas!

Raff, my deepest prayer is that someday you can forgive me. I don't deserve your forgiveness, but I hope you can extend it to me. I am proud of you, son. I wish I could be there to tell you in person, but God had different ideas. So, I pray that someday you will find Jesus too so that we can be together in heaven forever with your mother.

I love you,
Dad

Sobbing, Raff lay his head in her lap. Maddie stroked his hair. He got up, and Maddie held him as he sobbed until there was nothing left. No more tears. This ended a lifelong struggle in a way that was so wonderful, so beautiful, that he knew it was something only God could do.

Raff sat up next to Maddie. For a long while, they just sat there. He couldn't speak, and Maddie wouldn't. He finally handed her the letter and asked her to read it. She took it and read. When she was finished, she had tears in her eyes.

"Oh, Raff, this is what you've wanted your whole life. I'm so glad your dad wrote this for you. How are you feeling?"

"Um…well, I guess right now I feel sadness, happiness, joy, and sorrow all mixed up together. My dad loved me. I wished I'd known years ago, but God did give me this gift. Maddie, it's the best Christmas gift I've ever received." He smiled weakly.

"You have a reason to have mixed emotions. This is heavy stuff, but good stuff too. And yes, it was a gift from God. Just think, you will see your dad and mom in heaven and spend eternity with them and Jesus. It doesn't get any better than that."

"You're right."

"Raff, let's get out of here and go downstairs. I think we've explored enough and have inhaled more than our share of dust for one day. We need and have earned a break."

"You are so right, my sweet. We certainly have."

"How about we go to the café and get some comfort food? Something decadent and filled with calories. My treat."

"Your treat, huh? That'd be a first."

"Yep."

"Well, I'm not dumb enough to turn that down. You're on."

They got their coats and boots on and headed outside. Fresh snow had fallen, and the temperature had dropped again, but not enough that it turned everything to ice. They got into the car and drove off down the street toward town.

CHAPTER 42

"Loretta, get in here," Lucas commanded.

"Coming, sir," she said, rolling her eyes. Under her breath, she added, "Sir, yes, sir, general, sir." She walked through the door. "You needed me, sir?"

"Call Raff Mayfield and tell him to get in here—and to come alone. Make an appointment with him for tomorrow," he barked.

"Yes, sir. Right away, sir."

"Now get out! I'm busy!" he roared.

"Yes, sir, right away." She hurried out the door as fast as she could. "I've got to find another job," she said under her breath.

She sat at her desk and pulled the file out that had been sitting there. She dialed the phone, waiting for the ring and the answer. It rang for a long time, and she finally hung up. She didn't relish the idea of telling him that he didn't answer. She got up from her desk and knocked on his door.

"What is it!" he shrieked.

"He didn't answer, sir."

He slammed his fist on the desk and cursed. "Well, try again, and keep trying until you reach him!" he thundered.

"Yes, sir." Her chin was trembling. She waited a few minutes and tried again. It rang ten times, and she hung up again.

She knocked on the door again.

"What is it now, you idiot?" he snarled.

"He's not home, and it's after closing time, so I'm heading home. Good night, Mr. Sprat," she said, almost spitting out the words. She wished she could quit.

"Yeah, go!" he growled. "You're useless anyway. I have to do everything myself." He heard the door close.

CHAPTER 43

The next afternoon, Maddie knocked on the door, and Raff opened it and invited her in. She took off her coat and boots and sat on the couch. "So, cowboy, you got any coffee?"

"I do. Hold on a second, and I'll be right back with one hot cup of black coffee for ya." He left the room and walked into the kitchen. Seconds later, he came back with a cup and placed it on the table next to Maddie.

"Thanks. So, are you ready for another day in the attic?"

"Actually, I have a better idea."

"Really? Do tell."

"Remember when I told you about my visit with Strafford?"

"Yes."

"He had really studied the Christmas tree when he first came in the house, even seemed to extract some joy from it. It was slight, but I think I caught that smile, and maybe a short memory or something."

"Go on, Mayfield."

"Well, then I went back to the bathroom to get the prescriptions. When I came back and was walking into the living room, I saw him staring at the tree, and smiling. Even touching the tinsel. I asked him if he had a tree, and he said he wasn't really into it. But there was something in his face that told me that he would really enjoy one. How would you feel about taking a tree to him and decorating it?"

"I would love that!"

"Let's head back to the farm and find us another tree."

Raff turned out the light, and he and Maddie walked down the stairs, put on their coats and boots, and walked to the car.

"Wait, where are we going to get the decorations?"

"Let's go to my house. I think there's a couple boxes left over that we didn't use. Maybe we can find enough there to make it work."

"That's a great idea. Let's head there first."

"I love decorating trees," she said as Raff opened the door for her. He kissed her on the cheek.

"Thanks, Maddie."

"For what?"

"For telling me more about the Bible. I'm glad you know so much. It helps me since I know next to nothing. And I started reading my mom's Bible. Reading her notes is so insightful. I love that. I'm learning more about God and my mom at the same time."

"That's great, and it's my pleasure. I love you, Mayfield."

"I love you, too, my sweet."

Raff walked around the front, opened the door, started the car, and went on their way to the farm.

It was dark when they reached Mr. Strattford's house. The lights were on, so Raff knew he was home. They walked to the front door, and Raff knocked. A few seconds later, Miles came to the door and opened it, surprised at who was standing there.

"Raff, what are you doing here?"

"Hello, Mr. Strattford. Well, I've got a surprise for you. This is Maddie, my girlfriend."

"Nice to meet you, Maddie," he said as he shook her hand.

"Nice to meet you, too, sir."

"You have a surprise for me?"

"Yes, mind if we bring it in?" he asked excitedly.

"I... I guess so. What is it?"

"Just wait and see. Please leave the door open."

"Okay," he said, uncertainty obvious in his voice.

Raff and Maddie took the tree off the car and hauled it into the house.

"Where would you like it, Mr. Strattford?"

"You brought me a tree?"

"Ah, yeah. Looks like it."

"I've never had a tree before—not here anyway," he said, choking up a little. "Put it over by the window."

"Well, you've got a tree now, so let's stand it up and get it decorated."

"I don't have any decorations or anything."

"Don't worry about that, we brought them with us," Raff said, smiling. "You want to help us bring in the boxes, and we'll get this thing prettied up?"

"Sure." They walked out the door. "Raff, I can't believe you did this. Why did you?"

"Because I saw the way you looked at my tree. Later, Maddie and I were talking about your visit, and I thought that it would be a fun thing to do. Until this year, I didn't have a tree either. When I gave my life to Jesus, Christmas became a gift that I'll treasure the rest of my life, and I want to share it with as many people as I can. It changed everything when I found out that Jesus gave his life for me, because he loves me. That is the gift. The only gift that really matters."

"Well, I can sure see a change in you, and I'm proud of you, Raff. Real proud. This...bringing this tree to me is something I will never forget. It's very special." His voice caught.

They each picked up a box and headed back in the house. They spent the next two hours decorating and just enjoying the Christmas spirit.

As they were leaving, Miles hugged Raff, and with tears in his eyes, he thanked them both for coming and leaving the best Christmas present he'd had in years.

When they were in the car, they rejoiced together in the way God had led them to this man who was lonely and desperately needing a special touch of Christmas.

CHAPTER 44

Knowing he had to talk to Kathleen, he wondered how to approach all the things that were swirling inside of him. But he had gone through everything in his mind—the good, the bad, and the ugly—and felt he was on even ground now. He just hoped that those doubts wouldn't surface, especially when he was with her.

Today, he was picking her up and taking her to the cabin. It was about time she saw how he lived and if that may be a hindrance to their marriage or her living with him in the cabin. He was anxious about it but tried to quell the questions that remained in his mind.

He spent the day cleaning and making sure everything sparkled. He wished, for the first time, that he had a tree and some decorations. The cabin looked so plain. Why hadn't he thought of that before? He had found some candles in the barn in a box and brought some in. He'd put some on the mantel and on his long, oval kitchen table. *At least I thought of that much*, he thought. He took a last look around and made sure everything looked spot-free and perfect.

He got in the pickup and took off to see Kathleen. He turned the radio on and heard Christmas music, which helped some with the knots that were forming in his stomach.

"Please, God, please let this work for us," he prayed. He stopped. He prayed? That was the second time he had requested God's help. Was his mind changing about all that Bible and God stuff? Maybe it was. He knew that Kathleen was a God-fearing woman like Pearly had been, but would it work for him too? He needed more time to chew on that one, but not now. He had arrived at the estate. His stomach churned.

He knocked on the door. Seconds later, Hettie appeared with her broad and wonderful smile.

"Well, if it ain't Mr. Frank. Always good to see ya." She laughed heartily.

"Good to see you, too, Hettie." That woman always made him smile. She was a dear lady, and he genuinely enjoyed being with her. "Are you always so cheerful?"

"I try. What's good 'bout bein' down when the Good Lord wants us to live 'bundant lives and be grateful for all his many blessin's? Don't ya agree?"

"Not sure, but you could be right."

"Come in. Kathleen's waitin' in the big parlor. Can't wait to see ya, Casanova." She laughed. "Seriously, I'm as happy as a wart on a bullfrog, Frank. Ya two are somethin' together. Ya can't take your eyes off each other. You're in love, sure as shootin'."

Franklin laughed. "Hettie, you sure do use colorful language."

"Look at me, Frank. What other kind of language ya think I got in me?" She roared.

He laughed with her. He shook his head as Hettie walked away and motioned for him to go to the parlor. He walked in and saw Kathleen standing in front of the tree, just drinking it in. Oh, how he loved her. She was the epitome of femininity and loveliness. He quietly limped up behind her, put his arms around her, and kissed the back of her neck. All his questions and doubts flew away, and all he could think of was being with her—anywhere. She turned around and leaned into him as he lowered his head to her face; breathing near her face, he whispered, "I love you, Kathy."

He moved his face and stared in her beautiful eyes as she stared into his. He touched her nose and kissed it. He moved toward her lips and put his finger on them. Taking his hand away, he placed it in her hair and pulled her head toward him and slowly kissed her. He pushed away and studied her face and pulled her to him again. The kiss was sweet.

"Okay, as soon as I can speak, Kathy…" he chuckled, "I'll tell you what we're doing tonight."

She giggled. "Oh, Frank, I've missed you so. I love you, Frank, with every fiber of my being."

"My dearest, I've missed you too." He cleared his throat. "Do you realize what you do to me when we kiss? I can't talk afterward. You, my dear, take my breath away, and apparently, my good sense, too." He laughed.

"Frankie, just what do you think you do to me?" You make my knees weak, and I can't think at all. I just want more." She giggled.

"That's because you've got such good taste in men." He chuckled. She hit his shoulder and laughed.

"Ouch!" He rubbed his shoulder. "Can't you at least change shoulders once in a while?"

They laughed.

"Okay, slugger, let's go. Let's get your coat and boots on."

He helped her with her coat, and she slipped her boots on, and they walked out the door arm in arm.

Hettie had seen and heard their whole exchange and was very excited for them both. Shaking her head, she said, "They may be in love, but if they be gittin' hitched in two weeks, we better get some plannin' done—if they can concentrate on anythin' but the lovey-dovey stuff." She laughed, shaking her head.

CHAPTER 45

P ulling up to the cabin, his stomach doing flip-flops, he parked the car wondering what her reaction was going to be. He watched her as she took it in. She looked at him.

"Well, what are you waiting for? I want to see where I'm starting the rest of my life, Frankie."

"Are you sure?" he asked quietly.

"Well, of course, I'm sure. Are you going to open my door or what?"

Franklin opened his door, climbed out, and closed it. He quickly walked around in front of the truck and opened her door. Helping her down, she stopped long enough to kiss him on the cheek.

"Why, thank you, my dearest. Always a pleasure to get a kiss from my intended."

He walked her to the door. "Are you ready?"

"Franklin Atwood, why are you so nervous? What do you think I expect?"

"Truthfully, Kathy, I wished I knew," he said as he rubbed the back of his neck.

"Well, you stop that this very minute! I know it's a rustic three-room cabin with a whole lot of love that existed here before, and shortly will again. So, you open that door and let me fall in love with the place that held your heart for all these years!"

"Okay, my dearest, here we go."

He opened the door, and Kathleen walked through it. Her eyes darted around the room. "Frank, it's so charming. It lacks a few feminine touches, but I would expect that knowing you've been alone here for a while." There were horizontal logs that had been whitewashed. Three windows in the living and kitchen area—really one big room. Although Franklin had made the windows larger than most, Kathleen was sure it was Pearly who wanted the place brightened up with the whitewash. The kitchen cabinets were white, but few. The countertop was short but had enough room for dishes, while the round metal sink had a window over it looking out onto the orchard. The fireplace opposite the kitchen was large, and the mantel was rugged and beautiful, wide enough for some Christmas decorations and stockings.

"You really think it's charming?" he asked in disbelief.

"I do. Without changing the cabin, I would like to make some small changes, but, Frank, I would never want to lose the charm of this place. It's beautiful in its simplicity."

Frank took her in his arms and kissed her. "You surprise me, Kathy."

"Why, Franklin Atwood, that is an insult! I thought you knew me better than that. Yes, I come from wealth, and yes, I like being able to do things that money can provide, but the simple life is what I've always wanted."

"You're kidding," he said flatly.

"No, I'm not. Wealth complicates so many things."

"It also helps many things," Frank added. "Kathy, I own an orchard of only twenty acres, and it's a lot of work. I don't make piles of money, and I'm not sure how I'd feel about you supporting me."

"Franklin Atwood, that's the most ridiculous thing I've ever heard. Marriage is about sharing everything, Frank. If you're going to get all indignant and hurt because I can use money to help you out—us out, then you better just get over it, because I won't be able to live with that!"

Frank laughed. "Kathy, I admit you're going to take some getting used to. I will keep my bruised ego in check. I never want money to come between us. Our marriage is too important to me. But I promise, I think I can handle it, and if I mess up, I'm sure you'll let me know in that quiet, sweet voice of yours." He laughed. Franklin lit the candles on the mantle and on the table. He set a place for two with wine glasses, and brought the wine from the fridge, opened it, and poured a little wine in each glass. "Shall we toast to our new life in our new home?"

"We shall." They clinked glasses, and Franklin said, "To us and our new life together in this home."

Kathleen replied, "To us and our new life together in this home." They drank the wine as Kathleen was still taking it all in.

"Oh, one more thing. I will build another large room so you can have Hettie come and live with us. I know you can't cook, and heaven knows I'm tired of my own cooking. If she's willing and you want her here, I'm okay with it."

Kathleen's eyes watered. "Really, Frankie, you wouldn't mind? I mean, I could learn to cook."

"Uh huh, Kathy, I don't think we have that many years left." He laughed.

Kathy punched him.

"Ouch! You talk about me bruising you. You keep this up, and you'll have some nursing to do." He chuckled.

She laughed. "I can live with that. Okay, are you ready? I think Hettie would like new appliances, including a washing machine, a new large white sink, a longer butcher-block countertop at least another three and a half feet with drawers underneath, and at least one extra cabinet, and a large-enough room so Hettie can have a sitting area. A couple easy chairs, table, dresser, bookcase, and a small closet.

"Oh, and a coat tree over by the front door so we can keep the chairs for sitting instead of a closet."

"Done."

"I would like white lace curtains, mint, and dark-green towel sets, new kitchen towels, and new tablecloth. And we can use a tapestry couch and a wingbacked, floral chair. Also, a new bedspread or quilt and new bed linens. Floral, but not too feminine, and a full-length mirror. Would you be terribly disappointed if we got a new rug for the floor? Did Pearly make this?"

"She did, but it's seen better days, and you wouldn't hurt my feelings at all to get a new rug."

"How about another coat of paint? Would that be okay, too?"

"Done. Anything else?"

"Probably, but that's good for now."

He smiled at her. "Kathy, anything you want is okay with me. The fact that you even want to stay here with me is more than I ever hoped for. I'll do anything to make you comfortable and happy—within reason, of course. But you'd better see how Hettie feels about all this too. We could hire someone else if she doesn't want to move over."

"Of course. I've lived with Hettie my whole life. There's no one more humble and more wonderful than she is. She'll move over. But I still want to hold parties and events at the estate and have her run them with the staff and me, if possible. Maybe there will be times when we spend the night at my house rather than driving all the way home. But, Frank, I love you, and you will always be my priority—after Jesus, of course."

"Of course. I don't fully understand the God thing, but I think maybe I'd like to hear more about it."

"That would be wonderful! Frankie, what do you think about having the wedding right in our home? I can ask Pastor Ryan to come and do the wedding. I would like to have Maddie and her boyfriend, Hettie, and whoever you want. Just something simple and sweet.

"But I think we need to decorate this place for Christmas and bring a little color to this cabin. Get a tree. We need about twenty strings of lights, and new ornaments. Oh, and I can use the new ones I bought at that festival and put my new wreath on the door. We need some boughs for the mantel and more candles. Also, some greens on the table with three candles, and candles on the kitchen counter. I saw a holly tree out there, and that would bring in more red. We need red ribbon for the tree."

"I think I have some ornaments around. I'll look. I think I have an angel for the tree topper that was my mother's."

"That's wonderful."

"Maybe we can put lights around the cabin, around the perimeter outside, and around the windows and doors—outside and inside as well."

"If that's what you want, consider it done."

"Can we go shopping to get some things for the wedding?"

"Of course," he said, smiling. "I want to make this wedding exactly what you want, Kathy. Except we're running out of time. Do we want some help getting this done, or do you think we can do it alone?"

"I still have to get a dress and a few personal items and pack, and I need to order a few flowers: red roses for Maddie and me, you, Raff, and Pastor Ryan, and a huge rose arrangement for Hettie to take home for all the work she's done for us. Oh, and we need to get a marriage license, too. So, maybe some help wouldn't be a bad idea. Why don't we ask Raff and Maddie over to help, and then we can have dinner together? We need to ask them to be maid of honor and best man, too, unless you have someone else in mind."

"No, that's fine with me. Ah…who's going to cook?"

"Maybe we can get Hettie to put a dinner together for four, and we can bring it home. Even I can heat things up in the oven."

"Okay, I'll let you take care of that. So, we have them come over the day before Christmas Eve. Decorate first, then dinner?"

"Sounds good to me. Let's finish our wine, Frank."

They sat down and drank the rest of their wine. Kathy was feeling all "warm and squishy."

Frank wanted to kiss her again, but he felt she was too vulnerable, and he would not take advantage. "I think it's time to take you home," he said a little protectively.

The love she had for this kind, wonderful man was almost overwhelming.

"We have shopping to do tomorrow, and you need to have that conversation with Hettie. So, here's your coat, and let's get you home."

"But I haven't seen the bedroom yet."

"Not tonight, dearest. You're going home. Now!"

"Okay, let's go. I think I feel a little sleepy," she said with her head on his shoulder.

"Here we go. You're going to fall asleep on me again. Are you always so rude?" He laughed.

When they got to the estate, he helped her out of the truck and walked her to the door.

"Kiss me, Frank," she said sleepily.

"One kiss, and you're inside." He gave her a quick kiss on the lips. He took the keys and opened the door, guiding Kathleen past him safely. He looked down the hall and saw Hettie close by and nodded to her, indicating it was time for her to take over, and she did. Frank closed the door, walked around his truck, opened the door, got in, and drove off.

CHAPTER 46

Raff was still processing the letter the next morning, when the phone rang. He moved quickly to the office and answered.

"Hello."

"Is this Mr. Mayfield?"

"It is. What can I do for you?"

"This is Lucas Sprat's office calling with a message from him. He would like you to come in today to get those papers signed, and he asked that you come alone. Around two work for you?"

"I think so, I'll see you then." *Why did he want me to come alone? Because Maddie unnerves him—a very good reason not to come alone. I need to reach her*, he thought.

Raff called her at the bookstore and asked if she could come with him to Sprat's office at two. She couldn't get away, and Raff couldn't think of anyone else. Then he had an idea.

❅❅❅

As they walked into Sprat's office, Loretta's face turned ashen. Then a few seconds later, her lips curled up. *This should be interesting*, she thought.

She knocked on his door and said that Raff had arrived, conveniently holding back the name of his companion.

"Please, Loretta, send him in and bring some coffee for us as well," he said sweetly.

Raff walked in, and a second later, so did the other person.

Shock registered all over Sprat's face. When he could finally find his voice, he cleared his throat. "Mr. Strattford, what are you doing here?"

"Hi, Lucas, I just thought young Raff here could use a little help with all this estate mess, so I've been helping him out."

"Oh, I see. Well, I just have some paperwork for Raff to sign, and then you can be on your way. Raff, I have a pen right here, and all you do is sign right there." He pointed to the line with his pen.

"Shouldn't I read it first?"

"Not necessary, everything is in order, and your father took care of the details, so just sign, and you won't have to worry about it anymore."

Pushing the estate paper toward Raff to sign, Lucas had covered most of the document with other paperwork, so reading it was nigh on to impossible.

Raff took the pen and put it on the signature line and stopped. "Are you sure I don't have to read it? I could take it home and read it there so I don't have to take any more of your valuable time."

Strattford agreed. "I think that's a great idea, Raff."

Sprat tensed. Well, I…ah… I really don't like paperwork to leave the office, until it's entirely finished. It gets lost or torn up, or the dog takes a bite out of it. You know, just not a good way to do things."

"Don't have a dog. I think I can handle a contract without it getting lost."

"It's just not a good way to handle business. I must insist that we finish it here."

Raff studied him. He could see Lucas's eyes shifting, not looking straight at him anymore. He looked a little agitated, out of control. *This is going to be fun*, he thought. "Okay, if that's the way you want it."

"It is."

"Okay, Mr. Strattford, I think we can be on our way." The chairs scraped against the wood floor, and they turned to walk through the door.

"Wait, you didn't sign it."

"That's right. And I'm not going to—ever! Any lawyer who won't let their own client read the documents before signing them is hiding something, and I intend to find out what it is." He grabbed the document and ripped it in half. Miles took it away from Raff as he placed his hand on Raff's shoulder and turned back, saying, "And, Lucas, I'm going to help him. I've always thought you were a little oily, but this proves it. I'm comin' for you, Sprat."

CHAPTER 47

O n the way home, Raff laughed at Sprat. Maddie was so right about him, and he was so glad he took Mr. Strattford with him. "That was a stroke of genius, if I do say so myself." He grinned.

He was almost home when he saw a pickup off to the side of the road, and there was someone still inside. Raff pulled over and walked to the truck. "You okay, sir?"

"Yeah, I'm fine, but there's something wrong with the pickup, and I'm not much good with cars," he said.

He got out of the truck and lifted the hood. "You know anything about trucks?"

"Hey, my name is Raff." He held out his hand.

"I'm Franklin." He took his hand and shook it.

Raff looked under the hood. He looked all over, then said, "It looks like there's a small hole in this hose here. You could tape it, and it might last a while, or I could take you into town and get the part and bring it back and install it. What's your pleasure?"

"So, you're a mechanic."

"Yep. I worked in a shop up in Denver for a few years, and I really like doing it."

"Wow, I could really use someone like you on my farm. With tractors, and the mechanical stuff all around me, I usually have to hire someone to do it."

"Interesting offer, but right now I'm trying to save my own farm that I inherited from my dad, along with a big mess. I really don't have time right now to have a job, but if you're still interested after I get my feet underneath me, I think I'd like that. Well, should we go into town and get you fixed up?"

"I think that's a good idea. I don't think Kathleen would be too happy sitting alongside the road while I try to fix it. She's a patient woman, but not that patient." He laughed.

"Well, let's go then." They both got in the car and turned around, heading into town.

"So, what kind of farm do you have, Franklin?"

"About a twenty-acre pear orchard. You?"

"Ten-acre apple orchard."

They chuckled.

"It seems we have something in common," Franklin said.

"Yes, it does. Tell me about yourself. Are you married?"

"Funny you should ask. Kathleen and I are getting married Christmas Eve in our cabin in the country."

"Wow, that's less than two weeks away. Congratulations."

"Thank you. We're so excited about it, and neither of us can wait. It's just going to be very small. Pastor Ryan, Kathleen's friend Maddie, Hettie, and me."

"Wait! Maddie and Kathleen?"

"Yes, why?"

Raff chuckled. "Talk about a coincidence! Maddie's my girl-friend. She talks about Kathleen all the time. She met her when Kathleen came in to buy books, and they just hit it off."

"Kind of crazy, huh? Kathleen talks about Maddie too."

"It looks like we're about to be good friends, Raff," he said joyfully.

"I would like that. I don't have friends. Just a couple. But I would enjoy getting to know you better."

"Well, I'm pretty sure you're coming over to our house the night before Christmas Eve to help us decorate for the wedding."

"Oh, I didn't know that. That's great. Maddie and I have deco-rated quite a bit this Christmas. One more will be fun."

They made it into town and back with the part, and Raff fixed it quickly. Franklin thanked him and suggested the four of them have dinner at the café very soon. Raff loved that idea, and he couldn't wait to tell Maddie how his day had gone. It certainly was full of surprises.

CHAPTER 48

"Loretta, get in here!" Lucas shrieked! "Now!"

Loretta walked through the door, riddled with anxiety.

"Bring up some boxes from the basement, and hurry up! Quit dawdling!" he barked.

"No," she said, softly.

"What did you say?" he boomed.

"I said no," Loretta answered, gaining courage. "You have bullied me, yelled at me, swore at me, called me names, and many other things for the very last time. If you hire someone else, I will make sure they know exactly who you are and how you treat people. And, I have heard enough to know that you are dirty, and I'm headed straight to the police!"

"Oh, no, you're not." He slugged her, and she dropped like a sack of potatoes. He walked over her and went downstairs to find some boxes. When he came upstairs, he pulled her under the desk and started to take his files out and throw them in the boxes. He knew he was in trouble, and he had to get out of town fast!

He grabbed another box and threw more files in it. He didn't have time to burn everything, so for now, he would take it all with him. He went out to the parking lot, to drive his car in the front. He was starting to feel all those stairs and slowing down. He needed to take the least number of steps to get all those boxes downstairs. His mind was racing. *Where to go? As far away from here as possible.* He went back upstairs to the office and grabbed another box. The next file cabinet was stuffed with files. He pulled a bunch out, and papers dropped all over the place. He bent down to pick them up and threw them in the box.

He was struggling to take deep breaths; his anxiety and adrenaline were a bad combination. He threw more files in the box and went around the desk. That's when he noticed Loretta was gone. He cursed a string of words that would make a logger blush. He slipped on one stray paper and fell with his left leg twisted underneath. He tried to move it and yelped! He cursed. It's broken! Wondering how he was going to get up, let alone get down the stairs, he lay there trying to figure out what to do. He tried again to move it and get upright, but it wasn't working. The pain was excruciating. He couldn't even get close to a phone, and even if he could, he didn't know who to call. He heard footsteps and lay still.

Someone came into the room, and Lucas looked up. It was the sheriff. He sighed. It was over. The sheriff had a few men with him, and they took the rest of the files, boxed them up, and took them to the prosecutor. Lucas Sprat was finished!

The sheriff called Doc to have him look at Sprat's leg.

Doc Anderson came and gave Sprat an examination. "Just as I suspected, it's a compound fracture. You will need surgery and at least a two-month recovery period. I can clear my schedule and get you in at the hospital within the week. In the meantime, keep it iced and your leg up. Absolutely no weight on it at all."

"But how do I do that!" Sprat shouted. "I need pain pills—lots of them! Now! Ice isn't enough!" he cried.

"Here's what I can do for you. I'll put you in the psych ward in the hospital where you will get twenty-four-hour care and your very own security. You'll be fed great food, three meals a day plus snacks, and there will be nurses in and out of there to take constant care of you. You'll never have to get out of bed. There are ways of taking care of all your private needs as well as bathing. I'm not quite sure, but I think I can get D. Hendrickson to be the charge nurse on the floor while you're there. Great nurse. One of the best. I'll get an ambulance to transport you over, and then Hendrickson can get you cleaned up and into a hospital gown so you can rest."

"Nurses, huh?"

"Yep. Lots of them waiting on you hand and foot."

"Well, I guess it doesn't sound too bad. It's better than sitting in jail, at least for now."

"Okay, good. I'll get the wheels in motion so we can get you off that floor and get you comfortable."

"Fine, just get me outta here now!" he squawked.

The sheriff and Doc walked down the steps together. He turned to the sheriff. "Well, he'll be in jail in the ward, so you can rest easy."

"Doc, you played him like a fiddle, telling him all that stuff. You actually made it sound pretty nice, like a luxury hotel or somethin'."

"No one deserves this more than he does. He earned it. Just wait until he sees D. Hendrickson."

"Why?"

"He's about 6'4" and two hundred fifty pounds of pure muscle."

They both laughed.

"Just let me know when he gets his first sponge bath," the sheriff quipped.

CHAPTER 49

Raff was so anxious to tell Maddie about the day he'd had. The whole thing with Franklin, then Sprat. That was so much fun— to get him right to the point where he thought Raff would sign and then pull the rug out from underneath him. He probably shouldn't have enjoyed it quite so much, but after all Raff had been through, there was justification for it.

As Maddie knocked on the door, Raff hurried to answer. He opened the door and pulled her into his arms and twirled her around. When he put her back on the floor, he pulled her in and bent down and kissed her with all the love he held in his heart. He loved her so much. He kissed her again, and then pushed back. He took in a deep breath, blew it out, and shook his head.

"Okay." He took her coat and threw it over the couch. He took her by the shoulders and sat her down on the couch, then moved across the room and sat on the wingback by the fire. "You stay on your side, and I'll stay over here. That's the only way I'm going to be able to keep my hands off you," he said, chuckling.

Maddie laughed. "Thanks, Raff, for taking the lead on this, I really do appreciate it very much. I think we both want the right thing here."

"Yes, we do. I will try to keep leading, but it's getting harder to do."

"I know, for me, too, but it is God's choice for us, and we need to stick to that no matter how hard it is."

"Not to change the subject or anything, but have I got a day to share with you! You are not going to believe it!"

"Please, I want to hear everything!"

"It started with a call from Sprat's office wanting me to come in alone. I called you about that."

She nodded.

"I felt I needed someone with me, and guess who came to mind?"

"I have no idea."

"Mr. Strattford. I called him, and he met me in town. He'd never trusted Sprat and has become pretty protective of me, so I thought he'd be a great choice. And, boy, was he!"

"Go on."

"So, since he wanted me to come alone, I walked in first, and then Mr. Strattford came in. You should have seen his face! I thought he was going to pass out!"

They laughed. "This is good, Raff."

"Then Sprat didn't want to look me in the eyes, they kept shifting, but he went ahead and told me to sign it—that I didn't have to read it. Everything was in order," he said, mimicking him.

"So, I asked the scumbag if I should read it, and he said no. So, I played along and said okay and acted like I was going to sign. Then I took the documents and tore them in half, and I told him that anyone who would ask their own client not to read a contract before signing it was not on the up-and-up. Then Stratton said that he'd always thought he was a little oily and that now he was sure of it and was coming after him."

"Wow!"

"I know. So great! Mr. Strattford came through for me again. I really do think that God is watching over me."

"No kidding! I knew there was something wrong with that guy. I never trusted him."

"I thought he was going to explode!"

They both erupted into laughter.

"I'm sure by now he's in police custody. Mr. Strattford really told him off. It was amazing! And to think I didn't like this guy! Talk about not reading people right.

"Oh, and there's more than this to my day."

"My, you have been busy!"

"You have no idea. Anyway, on the way home, I ran into a guy that was on the side of the road with his pickup. Turns out he needed a ride to town to get a spare part. He has a twenty-acre orchard. So, we started talking. Come to find out, he's engaged and getting married on Christmas Eve to—drumroll please—ta-da—Kathleen Brennan!"

"You're kidding! That isn't a coincidence! That's what I call a Christmas miracle! This is amazing! I love Kathleen, and we were already going to the wedding because she invited us."

"Franklin invited us to the café to dinner with them very soon. Can you believe it?"

"You're right, you did have quite a day."

The phone rang. Raff got up and hurried to the office to answer it. "Hello."

"Raff, this is Miles. I just thought you'd be interested to hear more of the story of Sprat."

"Sure. What have you got?"

"Well, after we left, he apparently started throwing his files together and fell and broke his leg. Then the sheriff arrested him for fraud and confiscated all his files.

"Once the prosecutor is finished with him, he'll be looking at twenty years. There's a long list of victims from all over the state of Colorado. The thinking is that the court will decide to require Sprat to pay all of them back, with interest. And with a plea deal, instead of twenty years, he would probably get fifteen. The man was worth millions, so liquidating his assets would cover the cost.

"They are also investigating the bank manager for his possible business dealings with Sprat since he had been recommending him to everyone.

"Loretta charged Sprat with assault and battery, which is likely to add another year to his sentence. That means you will be debt free!"

"I can't believe it! Praise God. This is all his doing. And yours, of course. Thank you, Mr. Strattford. I don't know what to say, but you've have changed my life, and I will never forget it. If you ever need anything that I can help you with, please call me."

"Raff, it ended the way it was supposed to. That man was crooked as a dog's hind leg. If I learn any more, I'll let you know."

"Thank you again, and goodbye."

"Goodbye."

"Hallelujah!" Raff walked into the living room and picked up Maddie and swung her around again!

"That was Mr. Strattford on the phone. Sprat was arrested and charged with fraud. It looks like he may be required by the court to liquidate his assets and pay back everyone he's defrauded! All of it, Maddie! I will be out of debt! I think the people Dad owes money to will know they will get their money when the case closes, so they should be able to wait."

"Raff, that's amazing! God is doing great work here for you and your dad."

"Oh, one more thing. Sprat broke his leg, slipping on a paper trying to box up his files."

"Well, the Bible says that God judges evil, and that man is evil!"

"I still don't have living expenses, but Franklin is offering me a job to do mechanical work, so if I do that, I should be okay. At least until early spring when the orchard needs tending. But I'm pretty sure I'll be able to handle it."

"God answers prayers in miraculous ways. Remember when I said that the gift of Christmas is Jesus?"

"Yes."

"Who do you think put this in a box and tied it up all nice and neat in a big, red Christmas bow?"

"You are so right, and I am grateful beyond belief. I never expected this."

"God's in the business of the unexpected. He is infinite. We are finite. We can't begin to think like him. This is all his doing. You have witnessed a miracle!"

And a wedding in the not-too-distant future. Maybe? he thought.

"Maddie, let's get you home, and then I'll come home and go to bed."

"Okay. I'm tired."

On his way back to his house, his thoughts turned to marriage and the farm.

Was it too soon to ask Maddie to marry him? He didn't mean right now, but he was afraid of waiting too long, for both their sakes. Maybe he could propose the night they were to decorate the Atwood house and have an April wedding. Sounded logical enough, but he wondered if Maddie would think so. A proposal on Christmas Eve might take away from the wedding, and Raff didn't want that. Was it the night before Christmas Eve or Christmas Day? Maybe he should talk to Franklin and see what he thinks would be best. But he wanted to propose on one of those days and hoped Maddie wouldn't think it was ridiculous.

Knowing now that the farm would be saved was a huge relief. Once the debts were settled, he could start fixing up the house. It was in dire need of repairs, some paint, something to make it homey. As he looked around the room, he became aware of small repairs needed. But if he worked at it, it could be a nice house again. He didn't think it needed a total remodel, but the kitchen probably needed the most work. The countertops were in bad shape, the wood was rotting from years of neglect. He could do most of it himself and maybe get Maddie to help with the painting and cleanup.

Raff made a list of all he would need to begin work on the kitchen and living room. It would take some cash, but he might be able to swing it, if he did it in stages instead of getting all the supplies needed for the whole house. Raff headed into the office for some paper and a pencil. He glanced around the bookcase and then took a closer look. He looked at the books. Someday he was going to start reading some of these classics. He was glad he wouldn't have to sell even one to save the farm.

Speaking of books, he thought, *I never finished* A Christmas Carol. *Should probably finish and see how Scrooge actually made it through.* He had time, so he decided to set everything aside and just sit and read by the fire. He had always loved the feeling of a fire in the fireplace. Besides, chopping wood was great exercise and cathartic.

After reading for a while, he came near the end.

"I don't know what to do!" cried Scrooge, laughing and crying in the same breath and making a perfect Laocoon of himself with his stockings. "I am light as a feather, I am as happy as an angel, I am as merry as a schoolboy. I am as giddy as a drunken man.

"A Merry Christmas to everybody! A Happy New Year to all the world.

"I will honor Christmas in my heart, and try to keep it all the year. I will live in the past, the present, and the future... The Spirits of all Three shall strive within me. I will not shut out the lessons that they teach."

And it was always said of him, that he knew how to keep Christmas well, if any man alive possessed the knowledge. May that be truly said of us, and all of us! And so, as Tiny Tim observed, God Bless Us, Every One!

Raff smiled. *I know exactly how he felt! Redemption is a powerful thing, and that experience will stay with me for the rest of my life,* he thought. Scrooge went through a lot to get there, but so had he. He was glad that the letter his dad wrote made such a difference in the way he felt about him. It didn't erase it, but he understood it better and was able to rejoice with him in his decision to follow Jesus. He knew how it had changed his own life.

CHAPTER 50

Kathleen called Maddie and set it up for them to come over in the afternoon and decorate and then have a delicious dinner. She already knew because Franklin told Raff. But she didn't say anything.

When Raff and Maddie arrived, they could hear Christmas music. Maddie enjoyed that because that set the atmosphere for the whole evening. Christmas decorating. She was becoming a professional; she'd done so many trees and some decorating of her own home and a little in Raff's. This should be fun because there was the four of them. She was anxious to meet Franklin from the way both Kathleen and Raff talked about him. Raff knocked on the door, and Franklin opened it. They walked through the door, and Franklin took their coats and put them over the wingbacked chair while they looked around.

Franklin held his hand out to Maddie. "And you must be Maddie. I've heard so much about you from Kathleen."

"Yes, that would be me. Thank you so much for inviting us to help decorate for the wedding. It's so exciting. Raff and I have been doing quite a bit of that lately, so we should be able to get finished in good time."

Raff and Franklin shook hands, and Franklin introduced Kathleen to him.

"Good to have you," Kathleen said. "I've been trying to get together with Maddie like this for a long time. We've known each other forever. She knows everything about books and is so good at recommending ones to people. She's recommended a few to me."

Standing in the corner of the room was a naked tree.

Kathleen began giving instructions to them. "I think we should begin by decorating the tree. The strings of lights are in that box. There are some of Franklin's ornaments over there, with an angel that's from his mother to top the tree. There are new ones that we just bought, along with some red ribbon we can make into bows and maybe string some through the mantel. I also bought some home-made ones from the festival that we can use. That wreath can go on the door. The men can take several strings of lights to put around the house and around the windows and doors. Inside I would like lights, all around the room. Also, around the windows and doors. Then we have some boughs to put on the mantel and table and several candles to put all around the room."

"Okay," said Franklin. "All right Raff, grab a few strings so we can get these lights up before it gets dark. It comes early these days."

"Yes, it does," said Raff. He grabbed eight strings, and he and Franklin headed out the door. Franklin had all the supplies needed to place them on the logs and be confident they were secured.

Inside, the girls started in on the tree and put up four strings of lights and then started on the ornaments. While Kathleen was hanging ornaments, Maddie started making bows for the tree. She placed them carefully, making sure they weren't too close to the lights so they don't get burned or start a fire. Then she started on the boughs for the mantel. She liked how it was coming together. Then she added five candles, ribbon, and holly. She moved to the table and broke a branch into pieces and placed three tapered candles in the center with some holly wound around on top. The rest of the larger candles were placed around the counter. It would be beautiful when lit.

The men came inside to warm by the fire for a few minutes, so the girls had them start hanging the lights around the cabin. When they were finished with that, they went back outside, took more strings with them, and finally finished.

Three hours later, the house looked divine. There was candle-light everywhere and greens, lights strung, and the biggest of all, the Christmas tree. Everything was warm, beautiful, and wonderful.

Maddie couldn't help but wonder what it would be like to get married at Christmas. It was such a beautiful time of the year. She sighed. It was time to turn their minds toward dinner and help get it on the table.

Hettie had baked ham, red potatoes, green salad, and Christmas cookies for dessert. Coffee and hot cider were on the stove and ready, and the smells from the oven were fantastic, where Kathleen had been warming it while they were working.

Franklin had them all come outside to see how it looked out there. There were oohs and aahs all around. It was lovely. The spirit of Christmas was everywhere, and it felt like magic was in the air. It seemed to Maddie that a Christmas miracle was just around the corner.

Kathleen and Maddie set the table and plated the food without disturbing the arrangement on the table. Maddie didn't want to redo it.

Franklin asked Raff to say grace, and he felt privileged to do so.

"Heavenly Father, we thank you for this wonderful meal set before us and for our hosts who have been so gracious. We ask for blessings for Franklin and Kathleen as they get married tomorrow and that their joy will not be able to be contained. Amen."

"That was a lovely prayer, Raff, and thank you so much for including us. It was very special," Kathleen said appreciatively.

"My pleasure," Raff answered.

Franklin turned to Raff. "I know this is sudden, but would you please be my best man?"

"Are you kidding? That would be my honor. I would love to. Thank you for asking."

"Maddie, I would like to ask you to be my maid of honor. I know it's short notice for both of you, but everything moved so fast, we forgot a few details."

"Kathleen, I would love to. It's so sweet of you to ask."

"Nonsense. It's sweet of you two to do it for us."

They talked more about the wedding and Raff's events in the past few days.

"Franklin, I wondered if that job is still open. If so, I need at least a part-time job for living expenses. The mortgage will be paid, and when Sprat's case is over and the settlement comes, I want to fix up the house and rebuild the shed and start making furniture, which is what I love to do, but I need to work too."

"It sure is, Raff. I would love to have you work for me. And there's nothing that says we can't help each other come spring and harvest. We may not be neighbors physically, but I feel we need each other—us farmers. It's a hard job, and most people don't understand that. So, I'm here."

"Thank you so much, Franklin. That's amazing. I'm new at farming, so someone like you helping me is just what I need. I can't thank you enough," Raff said, smiling.

✳✳✳

Kathleen collected the plates from dinner and placed them in the sink. She brought the cookies and placed them on the table.

Raff looked at Franklin, and he nodded. Raff stood up and walked over to Maddie. Standing in front of her, he began to speak.

"Maddie, I have loved you even before I knew it. We were best friends, but in a way, we were more than that. We shared so many things in the tree house I built. I never told you this, but I built it for you, Maddie."

"You did?"

Franklin and Kathleen looked at each other. "Ah, isn't that sweet?" she whispered.

Franklin watched her and smiled. *Just twenty-four hours*, he thought.

"I did. When I found out it was you in that car and you were hurt, I almost panicked."

"You did?"

"I know I didn't show it, but I was really concerned. I didn't think I should show it. I hid my feelings until I couldn't anymore. Now, you know how much I love you, and seeing the joy on Franklin's and Kathleen's faces tells me it's time to plan a future with you. I can't imagine my life without you in it. We started as best friends, and now I'm totally, one hundred percent, flat out in love with you. Maddie, will you please make me happy and be my wife as long as we both shall live?"

He pulled the ring from his trousers pocket and opened it. Maddie stood and looked down on him.

Kathleen and Franklin looked at each other.

"Raff, I've been in love with you since I was seven years old. You didn't see me—not really. But we were best friends, and I died a little when you left. But I never stopped loving you. When…"

"Maddie, is that a yes or a no?"

Franklin and Kathleen laughed, and Franklin commiserated, totally understanding the situation.

"Yes! Yes, yes! You have no idea how long I've waited for this." They all laughed.

Kathleen and Franklin hugged them both and congratulated them.

"So, when's the wedding? And do I have to buy a new suit?"

Kathleen hit him again on the shoulder.

"Ouch! Why do you keep doing that, Kathleen Brennan?"

"Just love pats, Frank. Don't be so sensitive." They all laughed.

"I was thinking around April, if that's okay with you, Maddie."

"I'd prefer tomorrow, but I'll settle for April."

They laughed.

"That will give me time to plan the church wedding I've always wanted. I'm so excited. I'm an engaged woman—a fiancée. Such a fancy word, but much better than girlfriend don't you think?"

Kathleen agreed. "I'll help you with the wedding plans if you need help. I know your mom's been gone a long time, and if I'm not overstepping, I wouldn't mind taking that role for you."

"Really, you'd do that for me?"

"Of course, I didn't really have time to plan this one." She looked at Franklin. "So, it would be fun to help plan a church wedding."

Maddie went over to Kathleen's chair and hugged her. "Thank you so much. I would love that."

Then it was time for the dishes, and Kathleen and Maddie handled that in quick order.

Raff looked at the time and suggested they should be going. They got their coats on, and Franklin walked to the door and opened it.

"Congratulations, you two. I'm happy for you."

"Yes, we're so happy for both of you, and we can't wait to see you tomorrow night," said Kathleen cheerily. She was as excited as Maddie, but for a different reason.

"Good night, you two," Franklin said as he waved goodbye.

"Good night," Maddie and Raff said together.

Raff and Maddie walked to the car, got in, and drove off. Franklin closed the door.

"Wasn't that just the sweetest thing?" Kathleen asked. "Frankie, we both know what they are feeling. It's going to be a rough four months."

"I think Raff's got enough plans to keep him busy, and you can keep Maddie busy with the wedding plans and girl stuff. They'll be fine."

They both looked around the room visualizing what tomorrow would bring and wishing it were tonight.

"My dearest, I think it's time I take you home. The cabin is decorated beautifully, and I think there's a little too much mood lighting and romance in here. Do you really think I can be alone with you and all this?" He motioned with his hand around the room.

"Just one kiss, Frankie, please?"

"Okay, but just one, then we're on our way to your house. Got it?"

"Yes, sir, I got it," she said, pouting.

"Come here." He took her in his arms and stared at her, then kissed her on the top of her head.

"Franklin Atwood, you're not getting away with that again."

"Yes, ma'am, I am. No more tonight. Just twenty-four hours, dearest. Twenty-four hours. We have to wait."

"I know. I'll go get my coat."

"Good. I need to unplug the Christmas tree lights. I've heard of some who have had fires because the bulbs got too hot. Don't want that happening here." He walked over to the tree and unplugged the lights and blew out all the candles, then went for his coat. He placed his hand at the small of her back and ushered her out the door toward the truck. He helped her into the truck and closed the door. Walking around the front, he opened the door, sat down, and closed the door. He stared at Kathleen. *Just twenty-four hours.* He sighed, then started the engine.

Kathleen lay her head against the window and watched the world go by. Franklin glanced at her.

"What, my shoulder's not good enough for you now?" he asked, teasing.

She giggled. "Yes, of course, it is. I'm just trying to give you space."

"Kathy, please move over here and put your head where it's supposed to be."

She laughed. "Okay." She moved over and lay her head down. "Mmm. That feels so much better."

Franklin kissed her on the head and wrapped his arm around her shoulder. "I love you, my dearest," he whispered.

She was asleep.

Franklin smiled. He loved that she felt so comfortable and safe with him. He couldn't wait until tomorrow night. No more dropping her off and going home alone. He drove into the driveway and turned off the truck.

"Kathy. You're home," he whispered while kissing her cheek.

She didn't even stir. Franklin thought she must really be tired.

"Kathy, honey, it's time to wake up."

Nothing. He shook her. Nothing. "Kathleen. Wake up!" he commanded. "Wake up!" She was unconscious. Franklin started to panic. "Oh, God, I can't have found her just to lose her. Please make her okay. I can't live without her. Please, God."

Tears began flooding his eyes. He opened the door, got out, and walked quickly around the other side.

"Kathleen!" he shouted. He picked her up and knocked loudly on the door. "Hettie, open the door!" he yelled.

Hettie opened the door and saw the situation. "What's goin' on?" she asked.

"I don't know. She fell asleep on my shoulder, and now I can't wake her up."

Hettie led them into the parlor and motioned him to lay her on the couch.

"I'm goin' to get a cold cloth for her forehead." Hettie hurried off to the kitchen.

"Kathy. Kathy. Please wake up, darling, please? Please, God, don't let her die, please," he pleaded.

"Here, let's get this on her forehead. Don't worry, Frank. She's tougher than she looks."

Kathleen started to stir.

"Mmmm. What happened?" She looked at Frank and saw his eyes. "Frank, are you all right?"

"I am if you are," he said weakly. "How are you feeling?"

"I'm fine. What am I doing here?"

"You were unconscious."

"I was? For how long?"

"I don't know. I thought you were asleep. But when I got here, I couldn't wake you up."

"I do that when I get overtired or too excited, or both at the same time."

"I guess I better take note of that. You scared me to death. Please get enough sleep from now on, okay?"

"She's excited 'bout the weddin', and I know she ain't been sleepin'. Not eatin' good neither. She done that before. She jes' fainted. She be fine in no time. Gotta git her to the weddin' for ya two."

"Kathy, I need to know if you're well enough to get married. It's not like we've got a hundred people at the church waiting. We can reschedule."

She sat up. "Franklin Atwood, nothing or no one is going to keep me from marrying you tomorrow at five. You got that?"

He laughed. "Yes, ma'am. If you're absolutely sure."

"I am. Now go home so I can get some rest. Hettie will come over early and set up the food for you. It'll be ready to go before I get there."

"Okay, if you're sure."

"Now, you listen to me. I told you I was fine, and I am. I will never lie to you."

"Okay, Okay. I'll go home." Nodding to Hettie, he said, "Make sure she gets to bed okay. Can you sleep in her room tonight?"

"Yes, sir, Mr. Frank. Guess I better git used to callin' ya that all the time since I'll be movin' in before too long."

"Oh, so that's all right with you?"

"I go where Kathleen goes. Now, don't you worry none 'cuz I'll stay out of your way much as possible. Need to give ya space. Bein' newlyweds and all. That's all right with me."

"Good, because I think we'd starve if Kathy cooks." They all laughed.

"I'll get the men working on building it after the wedding. Shouldn't take too long.

Now, I'm going to get out of here so you two can get to bed and get some rest. Do I need to carry you upstairs like Rhett Butler in *Gone with the Wind*?" he asked.

"No." She laughed. "Then again, it wouldn't altogether be a bad thing."

She stood up and walked, a little woozy at first, but then totally on solid ground.

He walked over to her and kissed her on the cheek. "Good night, my dearest. Until tomorrow," he whispered.

"Until tomorrow."

Franklin grabbed his coat, put it on, and walked to the door and turned. "Hettie," he called, "if something else happens, you call me right away, okay?"

"Yes, Mr. Frank. No need to worry. She's fine and dandy."

He walked out the door and got into the truck and headed home. *Twenty-four hours, just twenty-four hours*, he thought.

CHAPTER 51

F inishing the list he had started for the materials needed for the house, Raff put down his pencil and paper. He turned back and looked at the titles on all those books again. He was anxious to get started on them. There was enough reading material for years. Looking closer, he saw that *Pride and Prejudice* was a little askew. He pulled it out a little more, and the bookcase opened.

"What the—"

There was a space that was about three-square feet and completely open. There was an open wooden box with a very old book inside. It was dark brown and included layers of dust for insulation. The outside pages were yellowed with age and looked very fragile. There was no title on the book at all. He looked closer. There was a keyhole.

"The skeleton key! Where'd I leave it? Upstairs, no. Wait, I brought it back down and placed it in the desk." He opened the desk drawer, and there it was. Grabbing it, he put it in the keyhole and turned it. It clicked, and the lock was finally opened. Now, to see inside.

He picked it up, placed it on the desk, and opened the book. There were a lot of bank receipts in it. It looked like it started with the sale of the horses. *Dad hadn't spent that money. He'd banked it for five years. With interest, there are thousands in here.* He could pay off the debt, remodel the shed, and repair the house with money left over. Then when the money came from Sprat's case, he would have more money to put into the farm itself and really turn it into something special. And enough to take Maddie on a really nice honeymoon. The good news just kept coming. God was working out everything together for his good, just like the Bible said. He couldn't wait to tell Maddie. He would tell her on the way to the wedding tomorrow evening.

CHAPTER 52

The table was filled with food, except for the food that needed to stay hot, which was still in the oven keeping warm: plain food, as Franklin put it. Turkey, ham, green beans, Russet potatoes, and gravy; Franklin loved gravy. For dessert, there was a two-layer chocolate cake, both Kathleen's and Franklin's favorite, and Christmas cookies. Gingerbread cookies, shortbread cookies, sugar cookies—all decorated beautifully, and peanut butter cookies. Franklin's personal favorite. The plates, silverware, cups, and napkins were on the kitchen counter, since there was no room on the table, and coffee and hot cider were on the stove.

Franklin had made sure that all the candles were lit, the Christmas lights were all on, and everything was perfect. Now that he'd done all that, there was nothing left for him to do. He paced back and forth.

The flowers had just been taken out of the fridge and were sitting in the sink. Hettie's arrangement was two dozen red roses, with a little baby's breath, and lots of fragrant eucalyptus in a beautiful hand-cut crystal vase. It was gorgeous. Maddie's nosegay was six red roses and baby's breath. There were boutonnieres for Pastor Ryan, Raff, and Franklin made of a single red rose and a sprig of eucalyptus, with a leaf for the backing. Hettie had already pinned Franklin's to his lapel and was ready to make sure all the flowers were handed out before Kathleen arrived.

Hettie had everything ready and was just checking on the details, when they both sat down, Franklin in the rocker and Hettie in the wingbacked chair.

"Are ya nervous, Mr. Frank?" she asked merrily.

"Not for the wedding, just seeing Kathy and making sure she's okay."

"She's fine and dandy, don't you worry none. She might wanna make a grand entrance, so she might be a little late. After the guests arrive."

"That's all right with me," he said, shaking his head, "but there's only seven of us altogether."

"Don't matter none. She been waitin' a long time for a weddin', and she should have a minute that's all her own."

"You are right about that. She has waited a long time, and I understand. Besides, that gives me a moment just to stare at her without drawing attention. Everyone will be staring at her."

"That they will, Mr. Frank, that they will. And I have to say you're lookin' mighty spiffy too." Frank was wearing a new navy-blue three-piece suit with a white shirt and a red Christmas tie. The red rose just gave him a finished and sophisticated look.

"Well, thank you very much, Hettie."

The knock on the door interrupted their conversation. Franklin was ready to get things underway, so he was glad someone was finally here. Hettie and Franklin both got up at the same time. Hettie turned to Franklin.

"Mr. Frank, I've been gittin' the door since before ya was even born. So, sit down and let me do what I always do. This's my house now."

Franklin laughed.

"Hettie, I'll gladly let you do whatever you want. You are a part of this family now. But if I get fat because I don't get up and get around like I'm used to, you will be held accountable!" Hettie roared with laughter.

Hettie opened the door, and Franklin followed, careful not to interfere with Hettie's sense of duty, to introduce them.

"Raff and Maddie," he exclaimed. "Come on in. This is Hettie. Hettie, this is Raff Mayfield and Maddie Henderson. Maddie is a close friend of Kathy's and Raff's fiancée—as of last night."

"Nice to meet you," Hettie said. "Let me git your flowers before I forget." She gave Maddie hers and then pinned Raff's to his new gray suit. "Mayfield. Ah, are you related to George Mayfield?"

"Yes, that's my father, or was until he passed away a few weeks ago, why?"

"Well, if that don't beat all," she said, chuckling. "That man saved my Kathleen from drownin' in the river a while back. He rescued her jes' a second before we lost her to that river for good. Praise Jesus!" She raised her arms toward heaven.

"My dad did that?" he asked in wonder.

"He surely did. In fact, he was so weak afterward, he stayed at the estate for a couple days. Not a good guest, though. Slept the whole time." She laughed.

"Wow, that sure doesn't sound like my dad," he said, looking at Maddie. "Except, he changed in the last couple years before he died, when he gave his life to Jesus, so maybe I can see him doing something like that," Raff said thoughtfully. "Thank you for telling me that, Hettie. It means a lot."

"We was mighty grateful that he found her, and always good to hear when another one finds their way to the kingdom," she said, smiling.

"Yes, it is."

Another knock on the door, and Hettie walked over and answered it.

Pastor Ryan and his wife, Sandy, walked through the door. They had never met Franklin or Hettie, so Maddie did the honors there. They mixed with Franklin and the others and were lost in conversation. Hettie got the flower for Pastor Ryan and pinned it on him.

"Thank you for coming, Pastor Ryan, I know it was on short notice. Mrs. Ryan, it's nice to meet both of you," Franklin said.

"It was my pleasure. I've known Kathleen for quite a few years now, and I wouldn't have missed this wedding for the world. She should be deemed a national treasure," he said, chuckling.

Franklin had no trouble agreeing with that at all.

"This is Raff and Maddie, who helped us decorate last night and are our best man and maid of honor," he said, introducing them. "And over there fussing with the food is Hettie, Kathleen's lifelong companion."

"Yes, I've known Maddie for a long time, too, and Raff and I have been talking. The three of us are having a Bible study together."

"Very nice. These two are great kids. Raff's going to work for me as a mechanic, and Maddie is good friends with Kathy." He glanced at the clock. "Speaking of Kathy, I wonder where she is. She's fifteen minutes late." The hairs on his neck stood up. Was she in trouble? Did she get worse? She's so punctual. "Come on, Kathy," he whispered.

Suddenly, the door opened, and everyone turned. Kathleen slowly walked in. She was radiant. Franklin gasped. She wore a white knee-length dress, illusion neckline, scalloped underneath. It was short-sleeved and fitted at the waist. Around the waist was a red sash. Franklin figured that was her touch for Christmas. The skirt was multilayers of white lace. She carried a nosegay of a dozen red roses. Her high heels matched the roses and sash. There was a necklace with a diamond heart around her neck, and she wore diamond stud earrings. Her hair was done beautifully, pinned up, with curls at the sides. She was beyond beautiful.

Franklin rushed to her side and whispered to her, "Kathy, you are a vision. I've never seen you more beautiful than you are right now. That dress is lovely. You are lovely. I can't believe you are actually going to become my wife any minute now. I love you." He gave her a quick kiss on the cheek.

Kathleen looked up at him. "I can't wait to be your wife. I love you, too," she said softly.

"All right, is everyone ready to get this wedding started?" Pastor Ryan spoke up, breaking the spell.

Franklin and Kathleen both replied at the same time. "Yes."

Everyone laughed.

"Let's get married, Frank," she teased.

"Sounds good to me." He smiled.

Pastor Ryan directed them in front of him and began the service. He began by reading 1 Corinthians 13, the love chapter.

> If I speak in the tongues of men and angels, but have not love, I am only a resounding gong or a clanging symbol...and if I have faith that can move mountains, and have not love, I am nothing.
>
> Love is patient, love is kind. It does not envy, it does not boast, it is not proud. It does not dishonor; it is not self-seeking. It is not easily angered. It keeps no record of wrongs. Love does not delight in evil but rejoices with the truth. It always protects, always trusts, always hopes, always perseveres. Love never fails.
>
> And now these three things remain: Faith, hope, and love. But the greatest of these is love.

Pastor Ryan continued, "Franklin and Kathleen, this is a higher love that can only come from Jesus. This is what he expects from us as husbands and wives. It's not easy all the time. It takes a love that we don't possess all by ourselves. Very high standards."

"Wait!" Franklin said.

"Frank, what are you doing?"

"I can't do this, Kathy. I can't marry you. If what the pastor just said is true, I can't love you like that. I love you, Kathy, but I guess my love isn't enough. You deserve someone who can love you fully—one hundred percent, and I can't. It's not in me." Tears welled in his eyes.

"Frank, don't do this, please," she said with tears flooding her eyes.

"If I'm to love you the way the Bible requires me as a husband, then I need Jesus. I've been running from God my whole life and questioning him. I just never thought he was something I needed.

"But lately, remembering Pearly and seeing the joy in Raff and Maddie, Hettie and you, I've begun thinking about it and have seen the joy you all have in God and the Bible. I would like to have that kind of joy, too. So, how do I get that, Pastor?"

"Well, it's not quite that simple, Franklin. First, you have to believe you're a sinner."

"Well, that's easy. After some of the things I've done, I know I am."

"Because he loves us so much, Jesus died on the cross to save sinners like us. We all sin, and we all need saving. The only path to God is through Jesus Christ, who paid the punishment for our sins when he was nailed to the cross along with our sin. God is a holy god, and as sinners, he cannot look on us. That's why he sent his Son, the perfect God-man. When we believe in him, God sees us through his Son. Perfect and blameless. Then we can live eternally in heaven with Jesus."

"I can't believe he did that for me. I don't deserve it."

"None of us do. It's a free gift. It is the gift of Christmas. All you must do is believe in your heart what I just told you and ask for his new life, and you will be a new creation. It is the miracle of Christmas."

"I do believe. Now what do I do?"

"Just pray."

"How?"

"Just talk to him the way you talk to us."

"Okay. God, this is Franklin. I guess you know that already. I'm new at this, so bear with me here, okay? I know I'm a sinner in need of a savior, and I know you are the guy who does that. I'm sorry I caused you pain on that cross, please forgive my sin against you and others. I want to love you and Kathy and others the way you want me to. I want to love Kathy with your love and all those things that are in that love chapter. Help me do that. Help me become the man you want me to be and the man Kathy deserves. I thank you for loving me even when I didn't know it and for never giving up on me. Amen."

"Welcome to the family of God, Franklin, we are all family now," said Pastor Ryan as he shook Franklin's hand.

"Praise be to God," Hettie cried. "Another soul for the kingdom and for my Kathleen. Glory be! Hallelujah!"

Everyone shouted, "Hallelujah!" getting into the spirit along with Hettie.

There was hardly a dry eye in the house. It was a very moving and unexpected event.

Kathleen threw her arms around Franklin's neck and hugged him. "I'm so very happy for you, Frank. This is what God wanted for you all along."

"I guess so," he said, smiling. "Pastor, I want to learn more about the Bible. I mean, it is a big book. Would it be okay if Kathy and I joined your Bible study with you guys?"

"Yes, it is, and you can never learn it all."

"That's for sure," Raff piped up. "It's okay with Maddie and me if you want to join us, right, Maddie?"

"Of course, that would make it so great for all of us."

"I can't believe how light and free I feel. And joy like I've never really experienced before. It's truly amazing!"

"Well, does anyone still want to get married?" asked Pastor Ryan.

"Yes, yes, I'm more than ready. Let's get on with it," Franklin said expectantly.

Everyone laughed.

"I think we were getting to the vows part of the wedding."

Franklin asked if he could say his own vows, and Pastor Ryan said that was fine.

"Kathy, I fell in love with you the first time you *bumped* into me just weeks ago. I have never felt a love so strong as I do with you. And now I know it will be even more so. I promise you that I will protect you, support you, cry with you, laugh with you, respect you, honor you, and always love you. I'll take care of you when you are sick. When sorrow comes, I will stand beside you and be your support, and we will grieve together. When joy comes, I will rejoice with you. I will always be faithful to you. When you walked into my life, you turned it upside down, and I think it will stay that way as long as we live. You surprise me every day. You say what you mean and mean what you say. You hold me accountable, and that says volumes about who you are. Kathy, I love you with all my heart. And I commit myself to God and to you and to our marriage with everything I have and with a love that only God can give me."

"Well said, Franklin," said Pastor Ryan. He turned to Kathleen. "Did you want to say your own?"

"Yes, I would, Pastor."

"Frank, when you bumped into me—"

Everyone laughed.

"When you bumped into me, I didn't have a thought about falling in love or marriage or any such thing. I had waited a long time and thought that time had come and gone. You crashed into my life and changed it completely. I fell madly, crazy in love with you, and will be the rest of my life. I promise you that I will support you, honor you, respect you, and love you. I will always give you my opinion but will defer to you as my husband, as you lead me. God will be the head of this home, but you will always come next. I will always be faithful to you. When we argue, I'll still love you. We'll talk it through. I'll share both joy and sorrow with you and will care for you when you're sick. You can tell me anything, and I want you to. I will stand beside you proudly for the rest of our lives together. I love you deeply, Frank."

Pastor Ryan nodded his head. "Very good. Do you have rings?"

"Yes," Franklin answered.

Pastor told them of the symbolism of the ring as a lifetime of love, not to be broken until death would part them. And the ring being of gold and not easily tarnished.

Franklin slipped a gold ring on her finger with a diamond in the middle and smaller ones on either side. Kathleen slipped a gold band on Franklin's finger.

"And with that, I now pronounce you husband and wife. Franklin, you may kiss your bride."

"I've been waiting for this all day." He took her in his arms and gave her a sweet kiss.

Everyone laughed.

"Allow me to introduce to you Mr. and Mrs. Franklin and Kathleen Atwood!"

They all clapped, and congratulations were said all around. It seemed to Kathleen that the whole earth rejoiced with them. She felt as though she could never be happier than she was right at this very moment. Someone had told her that the angels rejoiced when another human came to know Jesus, and she was sure that was true tonight. There had to be angels right there standing beside Frank and her. It was all too wonderful not to be that way.

Franklin told everyone to enjoy the dinner that was prepared for them, and Hettie made sure everything was piping hot. They all sat down but Hettie. Frank asked her to come and sit at the table.

"Mr. Frank, I've been servin' meals since before you was born, so don't go tellin' me what to do. Now servin' is what I do, so jes' sit down, and enjoy the meal and let me do what I was born to."

Frank shook his head. "Hettie, whatever you want to do is okay with me. I know better than to argue with you."

"Good, Mr. Frank. Glad we got that straight," she said, laughing.

Everyone joined in the laughter.

They sat and enjoyed the meal together. Christmas spirit was high, and the house was filled with wedding cheer. Everyone had a lovely time. Hettie cleaned up the kitchen while the others continued with their conversation. The pastor and his wife left first, and then Raff and Maddie. That just left the three of them—Hettie, Franklin, and Kathleen. Hettie left the kitchen spotless.

"Now there's a car waitin' for me outside. There should be enough leftovers to last a couple days. If ya need me to cook some meals for ya, just call me. And make sure ya don't let Kathleen cook. She'll kill ya."

They laughed together. Both Franklin and Kathleen thanked Hettie for all her work, told her to take her beautiful flowers, and she left the cabin.

They were finally alone.

"Do you think we could go to church together, Kathy?"

"Frank, I would love that. You talk about surprises. That's a big one. I'm so very happy for you—for both of us, really."

"So, you're not upset with me for stopping the wedding?"

"Good heavens, no. I'm thrilled. It means we can talk about spiritual things that you didn't understand before. Now we can truly share with each other. I'm so happy. And I don't think there's a woman alive who wouldn't want to hear how completely a husband wants to love his wife. That's frosting on the cake. I love you so very much, Frankie, my love."

"I love you too, my dearest."

The room grew silent. They sat in the quiet alone. Franklin in the rocker and Kathleen in the new wingback. Neither speaking. Just watching the fire. The silence grew awkward.

Finally, Franklin spoke. "Do you think you're ready for bed? I mean, would you like to go to bed, now?"

"I'm not the least bit sleepy. In fact, it will probably be hours before I will sleep."

"Well, great, because I'm not sleepy either."

"Then why—ohhh..." She smiled, a little embarrassed.

"Do you think you're ready? I mean, we don't have to tonight if you're not ready."

"Frankie, I've waited forty-five years for this. I think I've waited long enough, but I will warn you that at my age, I don't have the body of a twenty-year-old anymore."

"Don't worry about that. Neither do I. I'd say maybe we've been weathered a little, but I really don't care. I love you, and you are the most beautiful woman I have ever seen. If it will make you feel better, I'll stay out here while you change, and you can take as long as you need. I know these girly things take time." He grinned.

Kathleen giggled. "Not always, Frankie." She reached her hand up on his face and ran it along his jawline and threw him a bit of a "come hither" look. He grinned as Kathleen walked into the bedroom.

It seemed like hours since she had disappeared, and Franklin was getting restless. In reality, it had really been only a few minutes.

He unplugged the Christmas lights and blew out the candles, then he sat down again.

Kathleen walked out of the bedroom and stood in front of him. Franklin's jaw dropped. She was dressed in a white satin robe with a scalloped neckline embroidered with pink flowers. It was tied at the waist in the front and left loose in the back, falling all the way to the floor. He could see her shapely body through her robe. She was absolutely the most beautiful thing he had ever seen. Her hair was unpinned and fell below her shoulders. He could faintly smell lilacs, his favorite flower.

"Wow! Merry Christmas to me!"

Kathleen laughed.

"However long you were in that room was worth every single second!"

"Why, thank you, my love, I do dress to impress," she said, flirting.

"Well, you certainly impressed me! I didn't think it was possible, but you look even more incredible in that gown than in your wedding dress. I swear, you look like an angel. I've never seen anyone more stunning than you."

"Franklin Atwood, I do declare you are going to run out of adjectives," she said with a very Southern accent, truly pleased with his response.

"That's what dictionaries are for," he said flatly, as he perused the woman in front of him.

Kathleen giggled. "C'mon, Frankie, I'm ready to go to bed now," she said as she held out her hand.

"Kathy, you are my Christmas present that I can't wait to unwrap," he said with a smile.

Kathleen giggled. She took his hand and led him into the bedroom. Her heart sped up.

He took off his jacket, vest, tie, and shirt and put them over the chair next to his side of the bed and walked over to Kathleen's side and sat down. She sat on his lap and ran her hand across his chest and into his hair. She lifted his chin and kissed him long and lovingly. His chest was muscled and strong. He took her breath.

He looked up at her. "May I help you with your robe?" he asked tenderly.

She stood up. "Yes, please," she whispered, as she took a deep breath and held it.

After slowly untying her robe, he slipped it off and placed it at the foot of the bed. He looked up at her and pulled the covers down for her. He stood and kissed her neck and her shoulder, and finally her lips.

"May I help you off with your nightgown, Mrs. Atwood?" he asked softly as he kissed her neck again.

"I would like that very much, Mr. Atwood," she breathed. Her heart was thumping so loudly that she thought Franklin could hear it; she thought the whole world could hear it. "I love you, Frankie, my love," she whispered.

He lifted her nightgown then slipped it off over her head and ran his hand down her neck and partway down her back, sending shivers up her spine.

"You are so incredibly beautiful." He ran his fingers through her hair and down her neck. He stopped there and kissed it. He touched her lips with his fingers and then kissed them. He kissed her shoulder. He walked to the other side of the bed while she slipped beneath the sheets. He took off his trousers, and Kathleen saw the whole prosthetic for the first time. A wooden stump with leather straps attached to it that ran around his leg with wires, holding it in place. It looked heavy and cumbersome and painful.

"Please turn away and don't look. It's ugly. It makes me feel weak."

"Well, first, there's nothing weak about you, Franklin Atwood. And second, do you think I care one bit about your leg? If that were the case, I wouldn't be lying in our bed waiting for you to get in. I love every square inch of you."

"Every square inch?" he asked with a grin.

"Yes. Every square inch, and that is a part of you. So, please don't ever ask me not to look again."

"Yes ma'am," he said with amusement. He unwrapped the leather straps and winced as he disconnected the wires and put it on the chair and then got into bed.

She saw that pained look in his eye and knew he was hurting, but she decided to ignore it for his sake. "Frank, are you ever going to share with me what happened to you?"

"I will, but please not tonight, okay?"

He turned off the light and got into bed.

"Okay, Mrs. Atwood, come over here." He pulled her close to him, and then taking her in his arms, he kissed her with a passion he didn't even know he possessed—long, and like he had ached to do for a long time, only better than he had dreamed.

"You are so amazing." He kissed her again. "I still can't believe that you are my wife." He kissed her again.

He pushed away and stared at her. "Isn't it wonderful that God intended love to be complete in marriage?" he asked softly.

"Mmm, mmm."

"Merry Christmas, my darling," he whispered.

"Mmm, mmm."

There was a glow from the Christmas lights outside coming through the window that resembled candlelight, casting a romantic glow across the bed. He kissed her again, longer this time. The kisses deepened.

Franklin spoke softly, "Kathy, I promise I will take this slowly. I know it's your first time, and I just want you to feel…"

"Frankie, my love," she said softly.

"Yes."

"Will you please stop talking and kiss me."

He shook his head, chuckling. "Now, that's my girl!"

ABOUT THE AUTHOR

Cheryl lives in Washington State and is a firm believer in Jesus Christ. Her life mostly revolves around her family of two grown children, eight grandchildren, and nine great-grandchildren. Taking road trips with a best friend is a vacation that she loves, especially if there is plenty of room for Christmas presents. She shares her home with a mini–Shih Tzu named Cocoa, who's partially blind and a hilarious drama queen, providing hours of entertainment.

9 798889 433